PRISONER OF LOVE

CATHY SKENDROVICH

This book is a work of fiction. Names, characters, places, and incidents are the product of the author's imagination or are used fictitiously. Any resemblance to actual events, locales, or persons, living or dead, is coincidental.

Copyright © 2015 by Cathy Skendrovich. All rights reserved, including the right to reproduce, distribute, or transmit in any form or by any means. For information regarding subsidiary rights, please contact the Publisher.

Entangled Publishing, LLC
2614 South Timberline Road
Suite 109
Fort Collins, CO 80525
Visit our website at www.entangledpublishing.com.

Select Suspense is an imprint of Entangled Publishing, LLC.

Edited by Vanessa Mitchell
Cover design by Heather Howland
Cover art from iStock

Manufactured in the United States of America

First Edition October 2015

To my husband Rick, for helping me to create Jake in his image; to my son James, who helped inspire this plot in the first place; to my son, Timothy, for his encouragement during those writer's block days. And to my dad and sister for listening to all my plot points. I love you all!

Chapter One

C'mon, Luce, it'll be fun. A girls-only weekend. We can do manicures, pedicures, take walks along the lake, and dish about men.

As Lucy Parker drove along the deserted highway toward Big Bear Lake that morning, she hoped the "fun" her BFF, Jane, had promised would be worth the drive, the full tank of gas, and the unfinished office work she normally took home on the weekend.

Problem was, the drive was *boring*. Spotty cell reception meant she couldn't chat with her girlfriends to pass the time, and her temperamental CD kept skipping. Not that she really needed to hear the lyrics to the twangy country song—she was already living the refrain. Brokenhearted, down on her luck, and with a beat-up Honda in place of a pickup truck. Okay, so maybe her heart had only a tiny ding from breaking up with Jobless Bob last May. It had been her pride that had taken more of a dent, but still…she was swearing off men.

Bob had come at the end of an impressive line of losers and, after kicking him to the curb, Lucy feared she was more like her four-times-divorced mother than she cared to admit. Better to stop dipping into the dating pool while she was ahead and not end up like her mom: sour and disappointed with her life, seeking redemption in the company of Mr. Jack Daniels.

With *that* depressing thought circling in her head, she accidently passed the freeway off-ramp for the Southern California mountain resorts. Her second-hand GPS harped, "Take the next exit in one-point-two miles… Take the next exit in one-point-one miles…"

"Argh," she growled, looking for the next exit sign. She didn't know this unpopulated area at the mountains' foot. Her weekends never included skiing, hiking, or fishing. She'd never had the time for such activities.

"Take the next exit in nine-tenths mile…"

"Shut up. I knew I should have bought the automatic reset model."

She zipped past a roadside work crew cleaning up trash. Glancing at the workers clad in their bright orange jumpsuits, she figured they were from the nearby prison. That might mean there was an off-ramp nearby where she could turn around.

Finally, a sign loomed ahead. Turning onto the ramp with relief, her stomach dropped when she heard, "Take the next exit in two-point-two miles… Take the next exit in two-point-one miles… Take—"

"Oh, for crying out loud." Too late she realized that the off-ramp led to an interlinking highway heading east-west instead of north-south, with no easy way to turn around except for an illegal U-turn across the dirt median—and with the deep ditch at its center she had serious doubts about being able to make it up the other side. She was travelling farther away from her destination, with no solution in sight.

Lucy pulled over to the emergency lane and came to a stop, slamming the car into park along the deserted roadway lined on both sides with waist-high weeds and scraggly pines.

"Proceed forward and take the next exit in two miles... Proceed..."

In defeat, she closed her eyes and leaned against the headrest. "Proceed forward and take the next exit..."

This was a minor setback, she told herself. She wasn't lost. All she had to do was get on the other side of the road, return to the original highway she'd been travelling on, and—

The whoosh of the passenger door flying open snapped her eyes wide. A blurred orange figure blocked the daylight and threw himself into the passenger seat, roaring in a gravelly male voice, "Get the car moving *now*! And don't even think about jumping." He brandished a rusty file that had a nasty pointed end like a knife. "Do it!"

Lucy screamed. Just opened her mouth and let it rip, all the startled, adrenaline-rushing fear boiling up from her stomach like lava. The sound didn't faze the man beyond a widening of his wild, brown eyes. He grabbed the front of her black Hello Kitty sweatshirt and hauled her close, nose to nose. "Shut the hell up right now and do what I said." He stared into her face for several tense seconds. At last he shoved her away from him.

While Lucy cowered in the driver's seat, he kicked his left leg over the console and pounded on the gas pedal with his heavy foot. The car revved, yet remained unmoving, still in park.

"Damn it all to hell," he snarled.

His attention shot to the gear shift knob, and Lucy recognized the moment for what it was: her one and only chance to escape. Gathering the scattered shreds of courage within her quaking body, she slipped her fingers over the door handle, sucked in bolstering oxygen, and wrenched open the door, flinging herself into precious freedom—

Only to be snapped back into the confines of the ancient Honda like a Bungee jumper on a too-short cord. She hadn't unfastened her seat belt.

She turned toward the intruder. Her eyes collided with his and she saw her reflection in their shadowy depths. He shook his head slowly at her.

"That was stupid." He motioned with his knife hand for her to shut the car door and face forward. After staring into his sooty-fringed eyes for another chilling second, she complied.

He continued speaking. "Now, put this piece of shit into gear and drive until I tell you otherwise. And we'd better not get pulled over, because I have nothing to lose, and I'll take you with me in a blaze of glory. Do we understand each other?"

With no other choice, she nodded dully, shoving the shift knob into drive and punching the accelerator. Both their bodies slammed back against the car seats as they blasted off like a race car.

Oh my God. Oh my God. What am I going to do? Hysteria threatened to shut her brain down.

Oblivious to the life-or-death situation, her GPS decided

to continue its one-sided conversation. "Take the next off-ramp in three-point-three miles... Take the next off-ramp in three-point-two miles..."

The man in the passenger seat growled, "Shut that damn thing up."

Scrambling to placate her captor, Lucy tapped on the GPS, futilely pressing buttons while maintaining her breakneck speed. "Take the next off-ramp in two-point-eight miles..."

Without warning, her passenger slammed the heel of his fist into the GPS, splintering the cheap plastic and cracking its screen. Like music slowing on a carousel, the GPS sputtered drunkenly, "Ta-ke the n-next exxx..." until blessed silence filled the vehicle.

Lucy shot bug-eyed glances at the man while he examined a thin line of blood dripping from his hand. Raising challenging eyes to hers, he lifted the hand to his lips and sucked the blood away like he savored it. Lucy gulped and turned her eyes back to the road. She clutched the wheel while taking calming breaths.

Maybe fifteen minutes passed while they barreled down the blacktop. Every minute or so, she sneaked a scrutinizing look at the convict. He grasped the makeshift knife in one fist as his head lolled on the headrest and his injured hand lay in his lap. He seemed to be relaxing slightly, if his posture was any indication. Lucy hoped to memorize his features so that if—*when*, not if—she escaped, she'd be able to describe him right down to those sharply-angled cheekbones, the scraggly beard that hid much of his lower face, and that shaggy hair hanging over thickly lashed, dark eyes—

"Take a picture. It'll last longer."

She jumped when the man spoke and snapped, "That's so juvenile."

She half expected a hand to smack her in the mouth, or the dirty knife to gouge into her body. Instead, a rich laugh erupted from her kidnapper. "I'm sorry. I skipped the classes on social comportment in prison. My bad."

Surprised a little that his advanced vocabulary didn't match the rest of him, she said, "So you're an escaped convict."

"Of course I am. Did you think I was auditioning for the Great Pumpkin in this orange jumpsuit? Prisoner number 241053, at your service." He pinned her with another one of his penetrating looks. The tiniest flutter of awareness zinged through her—seriously, how messed up was that?—and she ruthlessly stomped it down. The guy might look more like a model than a murderer, but that didn't mean he'd hesitate to hurt her.

She pressed harder on the accelerator.

The convict leaned forward and opened the glove box, sifting through it as if looking for something. Seeming satisfied with his search, he snapped it closed, sat back, and spared a glance at the lifeless landscape blurring past them: fall trees with faded leaves trickling off brittle limbs, dark green evergreens stark against the cold blue sky and fawn-colored earth.

Lucy shuddered, realizing how desolate her chances were the farther she drove on this unfamiliar highway. She'd watched enough *CSI* and *Law and Order* reruns to know being a witness put her in a dangerous situation. Did he plan on killing her since she could identify him? Or would he hold her hostage? She knew as long as she was at the wheel she was worth more to him alive. But what would happen when they eventually stopped? She didn't want to hang around to find out. She needed to escape.

Wait! Her phone. In her purse. Fully charged. Another chance at freedom. If only she could reach it…

As if using telepathy, the convict asked, "Where's your purse, Pretty Kitty?"

Pretty Kitty? The comment had a major creep factor, but then she remembered her Hello Kitty sweatshirt and relaxed just a bit.

He leaned over the center console to peer into the backseat, bumping her with his shoulder. Then he dragged her purse onto his lap and pawed through her most personal possessions. With that final escape route lost to her, she was now truly at his mercy. She fought the sobs threatening to escape her throat as the convict pulled out the phone, his grin as gleeful as a child emptying a Christmas stocking.

"Eureka!" He brandished her cell. "Shiny little thing, ain't it, with all those girlish sparkles and shit?"

He shoved it into his front jumpsuit pocket, catching sight of her fear-filled gaze. "If you still want it, feel free to go fishing for it. Just be aware of what else you might come up with."

Ignoring the innuendo, Lucy begged, "Please, let me go. Let me call my friends. You can dump me on the side of the road. Take my car. They're waiting on me, and they'll be worried if I don't show up soon."

She held her breath and shot a sideways glance at him. He seemed lost in thought, perhaps weighing the merit of her proposition. Though he was probably just a few years older than her, the lines at the corners of his eyes spoke of a harder life. But then, prison wasn't exactly puppies and cupcakes.

Suddenly, he roused from his introspection. He met her look with a flinty one of his own. "As generous as that offer is, it's not happening. I need some down time and you're going to provide that by driving. I have no intention of hurting you. You're just a means to an end, so stop whining."

The convict reclined the passenger seat and settled more comfortably in the chair, closing his eyes with a nearly inaudible sigh. Within seconds his breathing evened out, enraging Lucy even more as she realized she was driving blindly with no avenue of escape.

As that thought crossed her mind, she lifted her foot from the gas pedal. "Don't slow down, sweetheart," her companion said without opening his eyes. "I wake up at the slightest movement. You learn to be a real light sleeper in prison, if you catch my drift. Now, how much gas do we have? I'm guessin' you don't go anywhere without a full tank under your belt, am I right?" Without waiting for a reply he added, "All I need is twenty minutes. You can handle that, can't you?" On a single grunt he eased back in his seat once more.

Swiping a shaking hand across her eyes, Lucy continued on her hurtling path into the unknown wilderness with a sleeping criminal by her side.

Chapter Two

Well, hell, hadn't he hit the jackpot when he jumped into this car, Jake Dalton mused as he studied the driver between slit lids. The only vehicle passing by on the empty road all morning had to be this POS. That sucked. At least the driver showed some promise, with that long ponytail of dark hair and all those curves stretching that pink kitty face on her chest until he felt like purring. If he could ignore her silent sobs.

Once he would have been ashamed of himself for bringing a woman to tears, especially one as innocent as Pretty Kitty, as he now dubbed her. After all, weren't cops, even tarnished undercover cops like him, sworn to protect and serve? Jake inwardly sneered at the thought of him protecting anyone. Hell, he hadn't even protected himself. His current predicament proved he'd lost the ability to defend himself, let alone the Pretty Kitties of the world.

Becoming one of the "wanted" had never figured in the

life plan he'd set for himself thirteen years ago when he'd earned his Associates degree in law enforcement. Raised by a single mom, the product of a drug-addicted father, Jake had sworn to clear the streets of the scum that had sucked his father into its depths. And after five years on the beat, when he'd risen to detective, he'd believed he was on his way. Too bad his mother died of a heart attack before she could see him at his zenith. Shifting in the uncomfortable car seat now, he acknowledged that the silver lining was she wasn't around to witness this current chaos he called a life.

Granted, undercover work gave him that surge of adrenaline he craved. That feeling of making a difference. When he and his best friend, Jerry Litton, also an undercover cop, began investigating suspected drug kingpin Anton Farelli, Jake jumped into his role as small-time punk Nicky Costas with enthusiasm. Almost immediately he caught the eye of Mr. Farelli, who pegged him as a go-getter, and Jake moved up in the drug organization, bringing the quieter Jerry along with him.

Everything went according to plan. Jake, as Nicky, worked the Farelli money laundering system between the Inland Empire and Las Vegas network, while Jerry remained more of a bean counter. Between the two of them, they gathered enough information to bring down the organization. But bringing in all the two-bit players in this enterprise wasn't enough for Jake. He wanted Farelli, the head of the snake, who always managed to stay clear of his own incriminating business. If they didn't get him, he'd just set up shop elsewhere, and more people would end up like Jake's dad, an overdose victim who'd left a wife and lonely little boy in the wake of his sad life.

Once the guys on the outside of the investigation deemed they had enough evidence, everyone, including Jake, got swept up and taken to county jail. It was paramount that he maintained his cover, just in case any of Farelli's people slipped through the noose. If that happened, Jake could continue his charade as Nicky Costas. A charge for narcotics distribution only lent him more credibility in the criminal world.

Following his "arraignment," he was moved to state prison to await trial, and received his work/training classification after processing. His captain, under the guise of a lawyer, had told him it wouldn't be much longer before he'd be cut loose like Jerry had been, so Jake had sat tight and tried to keep a low profile amongst the career criminals he fought to keep off the streets.

He'd lost contact with Jerry as soon as they'd been booked, but that hadn't been a surprise. Multiple undercover cops in the same lockup were just asking for trouble. What was a surprise was when, two weeks into his confinement, a group of Hulk-like thugs jumped him on the far side of the prison yard.

After beating him to the ground until he felt like a pile of pulverized carrots, one of them planted a foot in his chest, leaned into his face and said, "Mr. Farelli wants to know where his money is. You got twenty-four hours to get your shit together and tell me. You can find me in the laundry. If you don't, it'll be a finger next." The guy stood up and gave Jake one more kick in the ribs before saying, "Unless I slip and take the whole hand." They'd slithered away while laughing menacingly, with the tower guards none the wiser.

Since he'd been denied phone access because he'd

already reached his weekly call quota, Jake took matters into his own hands. Fresh out of the infirmary, he joined his road cleanup crew, and here he was. An escaped con. He had no idea what money those goons had been talking about, but he could guess. Oh, yeah, he could guess. Someone had skimmed Farelli's take before the bust, and Jake was the fall guy. And he wouldn't find out who really was guilty if he remained behind bars. Besides, he liked his fingers.

A muffled sob brought his attention to the girl beside him. His behavior wasn't much better than the bastards' he'd been rooming with. She was probably scared shitless. But maintaining his cover was the name of the game for now. So, while feeling uncomfortable with being the cause of her fear, he buried his twinge of compunction under a layer of nastiness that came much too easily to him.

"Snap out of it," he barked. "Jesus H. Christ, how's a man supposed to sleep with you crying and sniveling? Shit—Oh?"

He reached into the pocket where he'd stowed her phone and pulled it out. "My pants are vibrating, Pretty Kitty—"

Just like that, the girl rounded on him, eyes narrowing behind her thick glasses. "Stop calling me names! My name is Lucy Parker, or Ms. Parker. And besides, it's not Pretty Kitty, you moron, it's 'Hello Kitty.'" She faced front once more, chin quivering, hands and arms trembling after that out-of-the-blue verbal attack.

Wasn't that a surprise, Jake thought, staring at her profile. The girl hid more than generous curves under that ludicrous Pretty—no, *Hello* Kitty, sweatshirt. She had spunk. He would have liked that, as his other self. But right now, her feistiness only made her a liability.

"Thank you for clarifying my heinous mistake. I'd hate to be using the incorrect logo. It might give people the wrong impression of me, and I certainly wouldn't want that to happen." He stared at the screen. "When were you supposed to meet your friends? Someone named Jane wants to know where you are."

He couldn't miss the bloom of hope as it crossed her face, or the quicksilver smile that disappeared as rapidly as it had come. He felt the need to maintain the upper hand and squelch any expectations she harbored. As well as any remorse he still carried. "Answer me," he ordered.

She turned into a lioness, facing him once more. "Stop yelling at me! What do I have to lose? You're going to kill me anyway…I've seen your face. I can identify you. In fact, maybe I'll do you a favor and head for that guardrail right now, taking you with me."

The crazy girl in the driver's seat abruptly wrenched the wheel to the right. All of a sudden he found himself in a new life or death situation: his own.

She steered toward the edge of the mountain highway, a look of bleak determination settling over her face as she grabbed their destinies with both hands and held steady onto the wheel. Fingers of brush alongside the road blurred past as the scratched guardrail rushed toward them, and the blue, blue sky beckoned them to heaven.

"God*damnit!*" Dropping the knife and phone, Jake yanked the steering wheel the other direction, sending them lurching away from the rail and spinning back into the middle of the road with tires squealing. The girl screamed her disappointment, beating on his hands. The outside scenery careened past in an imitation of a carnival ride, while the smell of exhaust assailed his nose.

With him steering and her feet off the pedals, the car slowed next to the side of the road. The woman covered her eyes with shaking hands. Jake slammed the shifter into park then scrubbed his face with unsteady fingers before leaning back against the cloth seat.

The idling engine buzzed as he faced his not-so-innocent victim. That had been a close call. He'd seriously underestimated his hostage. Hidden beneath that voluptuous form and all that long hair was a fighting instinct worthy of his own. He had to admire it. Even toyed with the idea of coming clean, of telling her he was a cop. Shit, what he wouldn't give for someone to look at him with respect. Admiration, even. That was the problem with working undercover. You forgot what it was like to be good.

But, as much as he wanted to be appreciated for his real accomplishments, now was not the time. She wouldn't believe his story, anyway. He could cut her loose, though. He didn't need a hostage. She would only slow him down. And he sure as hell didn't need one as tempting as Miss Lucy Parker. She'd already taken him by surprise with that suicidal stunt a moment ago. He needed to keep his mind in the game, and not on what was under that kitty cat sweatshirt.

Opening his mouth to tell her his decision, something up in the sky caught his attention. Peering through the windshield, he spied a helicopter off in the distance. Shit. They'd actually pulled out a search helicopter for his escape. This day was just getting better and better. Now he had to go to ground, and take this woman with him, at least until his pursuers widened their net.

"I am not a killer," he said, with one eye trained on the

approaching chopper. "That's not what I was in for. After we get far enough away, I will happily dump you somewhere and you can go home. Killing you would solve nothing, although now I'm not so sure." He shot her another considering look.

She rested her forehead against the steering wheel, unaware of how close rescue was. Another pang of conscience speared him. He forced it down. He had to remain the bastard to keep her in line, no matter how repugnant it felt to do so. They were stuck with each other, at least for a while longer.

Heaving a sigh, he continued, "So, if you're finished with your melodramatics, take that turn up ahead. I need to disappear for a few hours until they're off my tail, and you're my wheels. Once I've had a chance to lay low and find my bearings, I'll be on my way and you'll get your life back. Now, drive."

He retrieved the phone and file from the floor of the car while keeping an eye on her and replied to the text from this Jane person. After pretending to be his captive and telling Jane something had come up, he apologized and signed off, hoping his answer sounded enough like her to prevent any more questions.

Without looking at him, the young woman put the car back into drive and continued up the mountain silently. Glancing skyward, he acknowledged that he'd finally broken her spirit. The thought turned his stomach.

She'd been driving for hours, it seemed. Once Lucy had taken the narrow mountain road her kidnapper indicated, the line of blacktop twisted farther into the mountainous, isolated terrain. She stared forward impassively, while trying to ignore the fact that she needed to use a restroom.

Just when she thought she would have to degrade herself more by asking to go relieve herself in the bushes, her captor pointed through the windshield. "Turn there, where that dirt track is."

Like an automaton she jerked the wheel to the right, plunged off the paved road, and pulled onto a dusty path barely wider than the car. How the heck had he found this donkey trail?

"So far, so good," he said barely above a whisper.

She continued up the steep drive, hoping against hope that a cabin filled with a loud, boisterous family would appear around the bend, ending her nightmare. Except then they would be in danger as well. Maybe a hunter's lodge?

A cabin did come into view after the next turn, low and rambling, made of wood siding with a dark shingled roof covered with brown and green pine needles from the crowding trees. It looked so obviously empty that she groaned her dismay out loud.

"Well, well. Not all my luck's been shit down the toilet. This is just what I was hoping for. And obviously not in use this weekend. Just to be safe, go around and park behind the house, away from view of the driveway."

The convict craned his neck at the cabin while Lucy slowly drove around back. A rusty, partially refurbished Postal jeep rested under the carport with bricks behind its tires. Cords of wood were stacked along the back of the place. Most likely a fireplace offered the only source of heat for this home away from home.

Before she'd even shifted into park her kidnapper climbed out of the car, stretching his arms and arching his back, Lucy's phone in one hand and his homemade knife in the other. If only there was a way to get either of those items out of his grasp. But how could she expect to overpower him, with his wiry frame and piercing eyes that missed nothing? She turned off the car and stepped into the nippy air.

"Get a move on," he immediately snapped, gaze lifting skyward. "No need to stand around out here, freezing our asses off."

What did it really matter? Lucy thought as she watched him study the gray sky. She was going to die. She didn't believe for one minute that he was going to set her loose. He'd just said that to placate her. She could tell the man was conniving. He'd searched her glovebox for weapons, plus he'd impersonated her via text to stop Jane from worrying.

No, he wouldn't risk his freedom by giving her hers. He'd kill her and dispose of her, perhaps bury her body in a shallow grave nearby. She would simply cease to exist.

The thought returned tremors to her body in full force, coursing down her backbone and through her arms and legs like pulsing electrical currents.

Raising her head, she found him staring at her with the oddest expression on his bearded face. An almost *apologetic* look. But then it was gone. He moved to the front of the car, opening its hood while abruptly beginning to hum a tune between his teeth.

She crept around to see what he was doing, maintaining a wide distance. What the heck? He'd pulled something off the engine. Oh, she should have taken a car basics class. At least then she would know what he was doing, although it wasn't hard to guess. He was rendering the vehicle useless for escape. He thought of everything, it seemed.

Her captor ducked out from under the hood and slammed it down with one hand, holding out the octopus-looking thing he'd removed for her to examine. "It's the distributor cap. Can't leave home without it." An ironic snort erupted from him while he tossed a glance at the postal jeep and its already raised hood.

Shaking his head, he ambled over to the vehicle. "Never leave the hood up for extended periods of time. All sorts of varmints will make a home in an engine. This one's already missing the battery." He glanced around the carport. "Oh, it's on the workbench. At least someone was thinking there. Know how to put one in?"

"N-no, I don't. Why?"

Of course she understood why. But no, she couldn't fix a car. She couldn't survive on her own in the wilderness, either. She hiccupped, the sound drawing a disgusted growl from him as he chucked her distributor cap onto the workbench and wiped his dirty hands on the legs of his prison jumpsuit.

"Christ, stop the sniveling. I already told you I'm not going to hurt you."

He opened his mouth to say more but Lucy blurted angrily, "Shut up. I don't believe anything you've said. You're a lying, thieving, escaped convict who…who probably overpowered his guards by…" Lucy cast about in her mind for something derogatory to fire at him. She couldn't come up with anything except, "Severe body odor."

Oh. My. God. *That* was what came out of her mouth? Seriously? Just how old was she? Twelve? And the kicker was, he didn't even stink, which she would have expected of an escaped con. Instead, he smelled like the shrubs along the road, the wind. Lucy wanted to sink right into the ground beneath her. With eyes scrunched tight, she waited for the knife he carried to slash into her body—

"That's all you could think of?" His voice came from behind her now, and Lucy's eyes snapped open as she spun around to face her kidnapper, air whooshing out in relief that she wasn't getting knifed.

He studied her with his head cocked, and she forgot to breathe as she faced his dark-eyed scrutiny. He exuded danger in every move he made, in every look he tossed her way. Yet for all his bluster, she was beginning to notice he hadn't done anything violent to her after waving that knife. Did that mean he wouldn't? Lucy didn't want to find out the answer.

Abruptly, he stepped back, took out her phone from his front jumpsuit pocket, and threw another considering look her way. "My apologies if I don't suit your obviously high standards. I've been slumming it for the past month or so and have apparently let myself go. I'll get right on fixing that."

His sarcastic comment, coupled with the unexpected humor glinting in his eyes, made her pause. He really wasn't fitting the TV and movie role of escaped criminal that she was familiar with. He should be yelling at her. Acting crude and coarse. But, except for his continued swearing, he really hadn't done anything else remotely violent. Which was puzzling, to say the least. However, the bottom line was, she was still his hostage. And she could never forget that.

Muttering something about having no bars, he flipped over her cell, removed the battery casing and battery itself before replacing its cover and pocketing the battery. Lucy felt like throwing herself to the ground in a temper tantrum, but she maintained cool while she watched her phone disappear into his jumpsuit pocket.

"Let's get inside and see what you can rustle us up for food, and maybe I can replace this monkey suit. Start making amends for my lapse in etiquette."

Then he grabbed her elbow, dragged her to the door under the carport. She tried twisting out of his grasp, but a quick jerk on her arm told Lucy he was serious. He pushed her against the wall next to the door and knelt to peruse the lock. Lucy made to move, but he stopped her, hand fastening around her calf, fingers digging into the flesh.

"Don't even think of running."

And just where would she go? She had no delusions about being able to outrace him to civilization.

He shot her a sharp look and she swallowed her words. Gone was the glint of humor of a moment before. In its place shimmered a touch of banked violence, letting Lucy know he was very unhappy with her behavior.

Immediately, she subsided against the wall, biting her lip.

His attention dropped to the lock once more. "Do you have a hair pin?"

After the silent reprimand she'd just received, Lucy simply shook her head. Heaving a long-suffering sigh, the convict rose to his feet and stepped back a few paces. "Guess I'll have to use my own personal password." He raised a leg, swiftly kicking open the door with one foot.

The flimsy barrier slammed against the inside wall, bouncing back toward them, and he shot out his arm to catch it. Turning to Lucy with a sweeping gesture and a half bow he said, "After you, my lady," and paused, waiting for her to step through the doorway.

Still recovering from the unexpected violence and wishing she didn't have to go inside, Lucy passed cautiously by her kidnapper and advanced into the cabin's shadowed kitchen, wrinkling her nose at the stuffy air of a vacant home.

The kitchen was a standard galley with gray Formica countertops, a dull, brick-red linoleum floor, and stained wood cabinets. A window above the sink looked out onto the carport, and across from the sink stood the stove/oven combination. There was no dishwasher, though a fridge crouched near the back of the kitchen.

Pushing past her, the convict flipped the kitchen wall switch and two pale ceiling lights that seemed to have time-traveled from the 1950s glowed weakly from above. Lucy stared up at them, surprised to find working electricity. On the other hand, the man appeared ecstatic, striding out of the kitchen and deeper into the cabin's environs, flicking wall switches as he went and commenting like a sports announcer along the way.

Lucy listened with only half an ear. Whatever he said wouldn't change her situation. Was this ugly, time-warped, abandoned cabin going to be the last place she inhabited? Would Lucy Parker ever be found after today, or would her image someday appear on an episode of *America's Most Wanted*? She forced herself to tune back in to his manic prattle, if only to bring her emotions under control.

"Holy shit. This place looks like a set from *Duck Dynasty*." Her captor poked his head around the kitchen doorway. "I've always wanted to hunt with ol' Willie. Get in here, Miss

Kitty. Quit your pouting." He held out his hand imperiously for hers, but she ignored it and just plodded into the dated great room, wishing she were anywhere but here in this cabin, with this man.

She had to admit that the plaid chairs with colonial wood accents, table lamps with huge shades, and an oval rope rug over a rough-hewn wood floor did indeed remind her of what the Robertson family might have lived in before they got rich. Too bad a real-life hunting family didn't live here. She might have been rescued by them. Unfortunately, the place was as empty as her bladder was full. Reminded of that fact, she blurted, "I need to use the bathroom."

Her kidnapper glanced down the darkened hallway. "Well, hell, I'm hoping it's down this way, although this place looks like it lends itself to an outhouse. Follow me." He moved down the hall with a purposeful stride, swinging doors open roughly and narrating, "Bedroom. Another bedroom, with more shitty plaid," and at the end of the hall, "Hallelujah, it's the head."

Light from a rectangular window over the toilet brightened the room, but it, like the rest of the cabin, had seen better days. Lucy stepped back, not liking the convict's proximity, though he moved out of the doorway. "Well," he said. "You hit the jackpot. A real bathroom with indoor plumbing. No litter box for you, Pretty Kitty." He snorted at his own lame joke.

Lucy didn't crack a smile. "May I?"

Her kidnapper waved her in, heading back down the hall toward the great room, saying over his shoulder, "Knock yourself out. But hurry up. I'm getting hungry." His voice faded as his body disappeared from sight.

That was when the idea took shape.

Lucy carefully shut the bathroom door and rummaged under the sink for a roll of toilet paper, batting away spider webs. Her eyes kept returning to that window, that rectangular-shaped gateway to freedom. What if she crawled out and ran down the hill? She might pass a motorist, or a bus.

She waited before flushing, debating her next course of action. If he heard the flush, he'd wonder why she was taking so long. For all his unpredictability, there wasn't much that got past him. She dropped the toilet lid down quietly and stood on top of it, shoving at the recalcitrant window to push it open with no telltale squeaks.

"C'mon," she whispered when her muscles met with resistance. Gritting her teeth, arms straining under the pressure, Lucy gulped down the sounds she wanted to express. *Just a bit more, it's almost there,* she mentally chanted as the window inched higher.

At last she felt it give, scraping along its track until the opening gaped wide. She put her hands on the sill, pushed her head and shoulders out so she could see the dirt and pine needles only five feet below.

"You can do this, Luce," she encouraged herself. The window was small and she had, unfortunately, an ample behind. But still her body made progress out the opening.

Until she got to her hips.

They wouldn't budge.

She twisted. She turned. She grunted and groaned. She sucked in her gut. Nothing worked.

Oh, why hadn't she gone to the gym more often? Why did she insist on double lattes with whipped cream on top? Because of that, she would die here, hanging halfway out of a bathroom window.

Her butt remained wedged like Winnie the Pooh's while tears of frustration, pent-up fear, and exhaustion tracked down Lucy's face and plopped in the dirt below. She coaxed herself to try one more giant pull to force her body through the aperture to freedom.

And then she heard the bathroom door fly open behind her.

Chapter Three

"Good evening, Michael. Come in, come in. That will be all, Sofia. We won't be requiring your services any more tonight."

Michael Delano watched the quiet housekeeper slip away as he stepped into the foyer of Anton Farelli's Las Vegas home. The older man looped an arm around his shoulders, and Michael resisted the urge to cringe. A hug from Farelli was akin to the kiss of death in the mob world.

"Sit, sit, Michael. What can I get you?"

Michael did as he was told, like he'd been doing for nearly two years, and sat in one of the gold velvet pub chairs facing each other within the gilt-colored den of the Farelli mansion/stronghold. Though his personal tastes ran more toward masculine dark woods and earthy colors, Michael decided the ornately furnished room somehow suited the mob boss, whose sense of style seemed stuck in the 1980s. Besides, who in the family was going to step up and tell their boss his home was garishly appointed? Certainly not Michael Delano. He liked breathing too much.

While Michael seated himself, he studied the glass-backed bar, noted the top quality liquor and crystal glassware reflected in the mirrors. He nodded at the scotch decanter his boss lifted inquiringly and watched him pour a couple of fingers before returning to the pub chairs and handing over the heavy glass. Remaining standing, Farelli raised his and drank deeply, one eye on Michael, as if making sure he followed suit. He did.

"Nicky Costas escaped from prison this morning," Farelli announced, turning and pacing the length of the sitting room. Michael blinked and quickly looked down into his glass while he processed this unexpected news.

My, my. Little Nicky had finally grown a pair. He hadn't thought the bastard had the smarts to come up with an escape plan, let alone follow through with it. Apparently he'd underestimated Costas. That was his mistake. Michael tuned back in to Mr. Farelli, who was still talking.

"According to my snitch inside, Nicky got on a road crew and just ran off, the stupid prick."

"Actually, that was rather smart of him," Michael ventured, but the ice-cold look he received withered the rest of his thoughts. He added quickly, "I say that only because it surprises me. I never gave Costas that much credit for brains."

Farelli stopped in front of the picture window that looked out on the fall desert landscape, indistinct in the evening twilight. He continued speaking though his back was to the room. "And that surprises me, Michael. You never miscalculate." He turned around, his expressionless eyes piercing.

"I want my money back, Michael, and Costas is my best suspect. It went missing after that last bust. Bring him here to me, alive, and I'll get him to talk. *We'll* get him to talk. And while you're at it, go check out Tommy. Even though he swears he saw Costas in the till when he thought no one was looking, it's Tommy who's wearing all the fancy suits and the Italian leather shoes." Mr. Farelli finished off his own glass.

An idea began to form in Michael's mind. "And what if they were dipping together, sir?" he ventured.

"I don't suffer traitors mildly, Michael. If you find out they were working together, make the one an example and bring Costas to me. I. Want. My. Money." His words, though quietly spoken, sliced the air like a scalpel. Michael nodded, mind racing to figure out how best to accomplish the deed. It would never do for Mr. Farelli to lose faith in him. He'd worked too hard for this position to have two small-time criminals ruin everything he'd built.

Hoping to forestall any criticism, Michael stood, a daring move as it might be construed as dismissive. "I've never let you down before, sir. This time won't be any different. I'll put a man on Costas's trail, and we'll bring him in." The placating words nearly stuck in his throat, but he was rewarded when Mr. Farelli clapped him warmly on the back, leading him toward the front door.

"I knew I could count on you. I love you like a son and I'd hate to see work come between us. Just bring me Costas and remember: if anyone kills him, they're as good as dead themselves."

"Yes, sir."

Michael stepped out onto the brick front porch, nodding

stupidly as Mr. Farelli quietly closed the door in his face. A guard emerged from the shadows, ready to usher him to his car, which he was sure had been checked for incendiary devices. Well, the clock was good and truly ticking down now, wasn't it? It was up to him to keep it from exploding in his face.

Jake threw the bathroom door open on a hunch.

Suspended at eye level hung the most perfectly rounded, heart-shaped ass he'd ever had the pleasure to admire. It wiggled and bounced, begged to be grabbed in both hands, held firmly, and either slapped or kissed. Maybe even bitten...

"Well, well, well," he drawled. "What have we here?" He leaned against the doorjamb with crossed arms. The butt in front of him wiggled in earnest now.

This was certainly unexpected. He hadn't thought the girl had it in her to stage this kind of desperate maneuver. It mirrored his own escape plan, though his had succeeded and hers had not. He grudgingly had to admire her daring nonetheless, even as he congratulated himself on checking in on her.

Enjoying the view a little too much, and loathe to remove that sublime shape from its place, he resumed talking. "I can just see the headlines now: 'The Grand Escape of Miss Pussy.' Probably would make a great title for a kid's book." As he stepped toward the clogged window, he muttered, "More likely a skin flick."

From what little he'd seen and felt, his hostage definitely

had the body for one. Casting one more look of longing at the sweet ass hanging right *there*, he placed his hands on the girl's shifting hips, allowed himself a quick squeeze before pulling her backward. She screamed all the way back into the bathroom.

"Nooooooo!"

The girl turned sharply in his arms, hair slapping him in the face, fingernails like kitty claws poised to scrape out his eyeballs. "Let me go!" Snapping his head back in the nick of time, he grappled for her wrists in a battle for domination, but Lucy Parker (oh, he remembered her name, all right) would have none of it.

Holding on to her was like harnessing a tornado. And all the time she sounded like the warning system for one, screaming and bellowing in his face. She twisted and turned in his grasp, that feminine form brushing up against him with dire results. Not that she noticed. Yet.

Their bodies careened against the bathroom door, banging it into the wall. First the wildcat tried to shoulder him in the chest, and then she stomped on his foot, screaming hysterically all the while. At last he bent her backward over the sink, momentarily gaining the upper hand. Their gazes locked, inches apart, chests heaving against one another.

"You're not going anywhere," he said. "Stop fighting. Oof—" He barely avoided her raised knee to his crotch, twisting his pelvis to the side at the last minute. With his unbidden erection, a connection would have dropped him to his knees. But the attack lent him the impetus to overpower the hellion, pinning her lower body against the counter with his.

She froze, her wide, frightened eyes latching on to his.

Ah, yes. His monumental hard-on. The sight of her ass and the ensuing scuffle in close quarters left him standing at attention nearly in her sweet spot. With difficulty, he brought his breathing under control even as his arousal raged on. She whimpered, not a muscle moving as she arched back against the sink, totally at his mercy.

He held her gaze. Debated once again about revealing his true identity just to stop this game of cat and mouse. But Miss Parker didn't look to be in any condition to believe him. "I apologize for my body's reaction," he managed between deep breaths. "That's not how I usually tell a woman I find her attractive."

He felt her start at his comment.

"I should have shoved you out on that highway when I had the chance," he grumbled before suddenly making up his mind and picking her up. He strode from the room with her in his embrace as she began screaming again over his shoulder.

He carried her to a bedroom. As soon as they reached the plaid-covered bed, she redoubled her efforts to break free until he flung her into the middle of it. Bouncing against the lumpy mattress, she bit off more protests while her eyes searched the room—for a way out or a weapon? He slammed the door shut with a shove of his arm. Then he turned to the knotty pine dresser, jerking drawers open and sifting through them roughly, all the while keeping one eye trained on her. She sat up on her elbows, poised for flight. In moments he found a suitable restraint: a pair of thermal underwear bottoms.

"No," she pleaded, crab crawling backward to the headboard, unwittingly doing exactly what he wanted her to do.

Fueled by self-disgust, he ripped the drawers in half and stalked her across the bed on hands and knees.

"'Atta girl," he encouraged. He knew he was scaring the hell out of her. But he needed to take control of this situation again, and she wasn't helping, not with those big, brown eyes begging him from behind her glasses, or that hasty escape attempt. Clearly, he'd underestimated her and he needed to expect the unexpected where she was concerned.

Good thing he did. She wasn't done fighting him. While he advanced toward her, she kicked out at him, nearly cracking him in the chin with one sneakered foot.

"Get away from me!" She swung her other foot at his head. Shit, it was like battling a windmill. Forgetting his remorse, he threw himself on top of her legs, making the headboard bounce off the wall and her scream even louder.

As he awkwardly crawled up her body she continued to try and unseat him, pushing at his shoulders with her fists and undulating her pelvis like Elvis in his prime. Which of course, caused another erection. He was coming off as some kind of damn pervert, when all he wanted to do was subdue her for a few hours until he could gather his thoughts and get the hell out of Dodge.

Ignoring whether or not she felt the hard-on, Jake grabbed her flailing right arm and secured her wrist to the Shaker-style headboard with one of the underwear legs before doing likewise to the other arm. At last he looked down at her and swallowed the painful stab of guilt at seeing her helplessly spread-eagled beneath him.

In retrospect, he figured he might have overdone the incarcerated asshole role. After all, his treatment of this young woman would likely leave emotional wounds and he was ashamed to be the one to inflict them. One look into her sad face and he hated himself. Hated what he'd become.

But the bottom line was they were stuck with each other for now. That sky-led search for him would widen overnight, giving him a window of opportunity in the morning to leave. And if he had to scare her into submission, so be it.

With a cursory nod of acknowledgement to the selfish bastard he'd become, he clambered off the bed and met her frightened gaze. "Believe me," he said. "I'd rather not tie you up, unless it's under mutual consent. But since you seem prone to flight, you leave me no choice. I need a shower, as you so delicately stated, and I don't think you're going to offer to scrub my back. I promise I'll untie you when I get out."

As he left the room, he heard her begin tugging at her bonds.

"Oh my God, oh my God," Lucy chanted to herself. Now alone, she redoubled her escape efforts. Jerking on her bindings, she kicked and squirmed, tried to break apart the headboard slats. But the knots were too tight and the old bed as solid as a spruce. Giving one, last, useless yank, she relented with a frustrated huff, dropping her head onto the squashed pillow and staring unseeingly at the ceiling.

She heard her captor rummaging through other bedrooms, probably looking for a change of clothes. When those noises ceased, she tensed, expected him to return to her room, but she remained alone. The sound of gushing water reached her ears, telling her he'd indeed started his shower. Slowly the tremors wracking her body lessened, allowing coherent thought to seep back into her brain—

"God*damn*it!"

Her muscles bunched as the vile invective exploded from the unseen bathroom. More curse words joined the first. She shook in anticipation of who-knew-what, until she heard the convict bark, "No friggin' hot water? This isn't any better than the joint, goddamnit all to hell…"

The swearing became hushed mutterings and the rush of water continued, allowing Lucy to relax temporarily and tell herself her kidnapper had gotten what he deserved. And while he was preoccupied, she took the time to contemplate her predicament, and the man who had put her in it.

She'd rather not think about her botched bathroom breakout—she'd been so close to freedom!—but her mind kept replaying the incident. And her captor's reaction. He'd been, well, harder than a bedpost. But he hadn't raped her. Or hurt her. Even when she was punching and kicking and scratching.

She knew better than to believe him innocent or incapable of violence. But she couldn't help but think that another criminal might have treated her so much worse.

Which brought her to the big question, why had he run in the first place? Wasn't that more a theatrical gambit in movies than in real life? You never heard about escaped prisoners on the news. Didn't most inmates fight their sentences in court? So what had made him so desperate that he couldn't wait? She found herself curious to know the answer.

She also wondered what he'd do with her when she'd served his purpose, whatever that was. He kept saying he wasn't a murderer, that he'd set her free, but why? If he hadn't committed murder, then his sentence couldn't be so hopeless that breaking out was his only option. None of it made sense.

With her head beginning to ache from her round-robin thoughts and lack of food, Lucy closed her eyes and willed her mind to go blank. All the willing in the world couldn't clear the jumble of thoughts flashing around her brain like a laser show. Her life as she knew it was gone forever. From this day forth, she'd be a victim of a violent crime, a name on a police file —

"I'm on the edge, the edge, the edge — "

She jerked out of her worries in disbelief. The man was singing in the shower.

Singing lyrics by Lady Gaga.

In a cold shower. Slightly off-key.

While his kidnap victim was tied up and spread-eagled on a bed across the hall.

Maybe she was the one "on the edge," because this situation seemed to be going from crazy to downright surreal. But before her mind could wrap around the absurdity of this rabbit hole she'd tumbled down, the water shut off with a grating squeak. Her body shivered, muscles contracting one by one. Even her fingers clenched uselessly as she counted the seconds since the water had been turned off...

"Are you calmed down yet?"

He spoke from the bedroom doorway and, looking at him, she strangled a breath in response.

The man straddling the threshold to the room could not be the same one who'd abducted her. This man looked like a male catalog model. He wore loose-fitting jeans and a blue plaid long-sleeve shirt rolled up at the sleeves. And he'd shaved. Gone was the patchy beard that had made him resemble a cousin of the Duck Dynasty clan. In its place was an angular chin and well-formed lips, high cheekbones and a blade-straight nose. His short, wet hair waved back from his forehead, with longer strands dropping over his eyes in an intriguing manner. Intriguing—what the *what*? She must've hit her head when they'd scuffled in the bathroom.

He plopped down on the bed beside her, his hip brushing hers. She scooted away as far as her bindings would allow.

"Are you ready to listen to what I have to say?" He looked at her seriously through those strands of sable hair.

She blinked, but refused to speak, still stunned at his handsome appearance. She would never have guessed the man in the grungy jumpsuit could be this...appealing. She squeezed her eyes shut.

Beside her he heaved an exaggerated sigh. "We've gotten off on the wrong foot, and I'm sorry for that."

This was just too much. "*Gotten off on the wrong foot? Are you serious? Are you even from this planet?* You barge into my car, threaten me with a knife, force me to drive you to this Godforsaken cabin, tie me to a bed, call me names, and then have the nerve to say 'we got off on the wrong foot'? To apologize? Do you really think 'I'm sorry' is going to fix this? You belong in the looney bin, not prison."

She glared at him after this outburst and jerked on the underwear bottoms tied around her wrists. He stared back, and she was surprised to see shame, guilt, regret—a whole slew of emotions flicker across his features like a montage on a movie screen.

"Okay, so I see your point—" At last, he lowered his gaze, reached across her body, and began untying her bindings. "I've told you before. You're in no danger from me."

She opened her mouth to spout off something about no honor among thieves, but his under-the-breath curse forestalled her. That, and the searching look he shot her.

"How the hell did this happen? I tied you with long underwear, for Chrissake, not barbed wire."

Lucy's gaze dropped to her left wrist, the one he'd released, and was shocked to see raw skin where her restraint had been. She hadn't realized she'd yanked that hard to get free. When he reached out and traced the burn-mark with one gentle forefinger, she couldn't control the shiver of anticipation that skimmed through her, or how her stomach flipped from that simple caress.

Crazy. OMG, she was certifiable. They had a term for this ridiculous kind of reaction. Stocking, no, Stockton. Shoot, she couldn't think with him this close and...caressing her.

His testing fingers moved as lightly as a lover's along her lacerated skin, over and over, until Lucy's insides wiggled like soft-set Jell-O. She found her attention captivated by his touch, and almost cried out in dismay when it abruptly stopped. Her eyes snapped up to his and she jolted from what she saw in them.

Regret, yes. Apology, also. But still more, she saw the flare of attraction. Desire, even. And was equally shocked that she felt it as well.

Chapter Four

She didn't want him to stop touching her. Jake knew this as clearly as if Lucy had said the words. He could read it in her face, in the way she caught her breath. In the way her cheeks flushed pink as the seconds ticked by. And he didn't want to stop.

Her skin was soft under his fingertips, beguiling in its smoothness, and in another time or place, he wouldn't have resisted. He would've run his hand along her arm, leaned in to kiss those supple lips. Would have buried his nose in the hair at her neck, breathed in that utterly female smell of desire he could already sense from her. But he couldn't.

He couldn't because he was her kidnapper. The man who had commandeered her car and her life just a few short hours ago. Even though he was an undercover cop, she didn't know that, and couldn't know that. Blowing his cover was not an option. Not if he wanted to survive.

So, instead of doing what his body and her eyes so

wanted him to do, which was sample what she didn't even know she offered, he brusquely reached across her and untied her right hand. At the sight of that abraded wrist, he suppressed his grimace and sat back, creating more needed space between them. Once he had her attention, he spoke conversationally, as if the sensually charged moment had never happened.

"There are two ways we can handle tonight. One, I can keep you tied up until I leave tomorrow, a rather uncomfortable state of affairs for you, from the look of it. Or two, you can give me your word that you won't try any more dramatic escape maneuvers, and we can pass a reasonably comfortable evening."

He could see her weighing her options. Flight, fight, or cooperate? He swallowed the ill-timed grin at her transparent emotions. She really was an open book, or else he was just too jaded. He feared the latter.

"H—how do I know you won't go back on your word? You're a criminal, after all."

Yes, indeed. For now, at least, he was. The knowledge soured his response. "You don't have to have a record to be a liar. Surely even Miss Innocent You knows that."

"Stop calling me names," she snapped. Obviously, his being a criminal didn't affect her spirit much. He found he liked the fact that she wasn't truly afraid of him, even if it meant he had to remain on his toes around her. As well as tamp down his improper attraction. She barreled on. "If you want my word, treat me with respect. Believe me, I could come up with a few names for you, but I refrain from saying them. Grant me the same courtesy, if you even know what that means."

Christ, he felt himself harden just from her gutsy retort. He really needed to get himself under control. She was supposed to become an unfortunate blip on his memory, not an ingrained image in his mind. In his thoughts.

So he took the high road, hoping a gentlemanly response would remind the rest of his body she was off-limits. Fat chance. "My apologies. My zeal over my successful escape overrode my good manners momentarily. Now, do we have a deal?"

Her eyes narrowed on his face. As long as she didn't look lower, he was safe. "You have a deal," she finally answered.

That *deal* didn't extend to dinner, Jake found out later that afternoon.

Of course she wouldn't cook for him, he reflected with some amusement as he banged around in the kitchen. He may have calmed her down with his more appropriate behavior, but there was no way she would wait on him. That was just as well. He didn't want to be too close to her if he could help it. Not when his body reacted to her presence like a metal detector at the U.S. Mint.

So, while she sat reading *The Sun Also Rises* before the fire he'd started, he rooted around in the kitchen cupboards before finding some family-sized cans of chili. Happy to once more be cooking, work he truly loved, he'd searched for anything else he could use to lift their meal from the ordinary. There was something about the rhythm of cooking, the soothing choreography of preparing a meal and maneuvering around the kitchen that sent him back in time, back to before his life had become a train wreck of impossible choices.

Puttering in the kitchen reminded him of when he'd invited a woman into his home and cooked for her, learned about her hopes and dreams through casual conversation before a roaring fire. Where he shared his motivations and interests over a good glass of wine and a gourmet meal, in hopes of finding that spark, that intense attraction that went beyond sex, beyond mutual compatibility. That fusion of body and soul between two people that lasted a lifetime.

Jake snorted at his fanciful musings and stirred the chili with more force than necessary. He hadn't found it yet in his nearly thirty-four years, maybe because he'd always put the job first and relationships second. Besides, it wasn't likely to happen to the product of a deadbeat, druggie dad and a single mom who worked herself right into a heart attack.

But he'd still searched, still hoped to meet that special someone, right up until he'd gone deep undercover. He'd even planned to get out of the covert business after this Farelli investigation. It had begun to take its toll on his mind, on his outlook on life, and he was wise enough to know when he was used up. Though it looked like he'd taken on one assignment too many.

With someone's well-placed whisper, his life had been tipped bottom-side up. Instead of being the predator, he'd become the prey. To make it even more challenging, he was working without a net. No phone service up here in this cabin meant he still couldn't contact his superior. He was on the run from an angry drug dealer and AWOL from the department he worked for. And he was thinking about romantic, fireside dinners with his *captive*? Jesus, he needed his head examined.

But he couldn't stop the inclination. Not with those big, doe eyes behind her glasses watching his every move and the way she filled out that ridiculous sweatshirt. No, he couldn't help but think about spending time with Lucy as a normal man might. Though not just because he found her hotter than the four-alarm chili he was known for. He liked being in the sphere of another person who wasn't an immediate threat. An ordinary person, with everyday problems. It was all the normalcy and little things in life that she represented—she made him feel...human, again.

Once they finished the meal and he'd stowed the leftovers, he flung himself into the plaid wingback across from the checkered couch she occupied. He picked up the TV remote and pointed it at the circa 1990s console set, but nothing happened when he pressed the power button. Either the batteries in the tuner were dead or, more likely, there was no cable. He'd have to wait for news of his escape.

Turning to Lucy, he attempted some of that commonplace, after-dinner small talk he craved. "What's the book?"

She'd been watching his every move, and still held the tome before her like a shield, drawing his attention to her breasts. He swallowed hard.

"Hemingway. *The Sun Also Rises*." She said it like she didn't expect him to know it from *Curious George*.

"Hmmm. Bullfighting. Ex-pats Jake and Lady Brett."

"You've read Hemingway." She quirked a brow.

"You're surprised." He allowed himself a satisfied grin, immensely enjoying impressing an attractive woman, even if she was his hostage. "You shouldn't be. Surprised, that is," he continued. "There's a shitload of free time in prison. Might as well use it to better yourself." He could tell she was wondering that if this was better, what had he been like before? What had he been like, indeed?

Swiping his hair off his forehead, he leaned forward and held out a hand. "My name's Jake, just like in the book." He had to say it. His real name. After all this time, after being swallowed whole by his undercover persona, he had to be Jake, just Jake, at least for tonight. He had to convince himself he still existed, if only for a little while. "I, uh, usually go by my middle name. Nicky."

His arm remained outstretched. She continued clutching the paperback, staring at him, unblinking. At last her gaze lowered to his outstretched hand, and she asked carefully, "Why'd you break out of prison?"

Here was the perfect moment to come clean. To burst forth and say, "I'm an undercover cop who's on the run for his life." He even opened his mouth to speak those words, to see her suspicion change to relief. Perhaps even admiration. He pressed his lips together. *Yeah, right.* Like she'd believe the word of the man who'd kidnapped her, held her at knifepoint, and verbally disrespected her. Besides, he couldn't tell her anything. The whole idea behind remaining in prison had been to protect his cover, small-time crook Nicky Costas. Until he actually walked away from undercover work for good, maintaining his cover persona was Jake's only security.

If Lucy ran to the authorities and told them he'd said he was a cop (and she would, he already knew that about her), all hell would break loose. The media would get involved, as they always managed to, and his ass would be fried. Once it was known that Nicky was really a cop, Farelli would put a price on his head. He was not the kind of man who went down without a fight. Hell, if his beatdown in jail had been any indication, there already was a price on his head.

No, even if he was tired of the subterfuge, Jake knew he needed to go out on his own terms. Not because some drug kingpin was chasing him into retirement. Or death.

As much as he hated playing the on-the-run asshole in front of a woman he found attractive and oddly endearing, she was better off reporting she'd been abducted by Nicky Costas and then dumped after he'd gotten far enough away. Of course, that also came with its own set of risks for Lucy. If her name as a witness somehow leaked to the press, and Farelli caught wind of it, he could send thugs out to pay her a visit. It would be best for both of them if Jake talked her out of reporting her abduction to the cops.

Fat chance.

But it was worth a try, as was attempting to raise her regrettably low opinion of him right now. Oh, he'd seen her do a double take when he'd returned from the shower. He'd felt her start when he touched her wrists. She wasn't immune to him any more than he was to her. And he needed to make that work in his (and in the long run, her) favor.

"The drug dealer I worked for put a hit out on me. It seems somebody told him I was skimming his profits."

Other than hissing in a breath at his bald answer, she didn't seem too torn up about one criminal planning on snuffing another. He needed to work harder to gain her sympathy. And cooperation.

"Were you?"

"Hell, no." At least his indignation was real. "But someone had to have been, because Farelli doesn't make wild accusations. And whoever it was pointed the finger at me."

"And you broke out of prison to—"

"To save my ass by finding the real culprit." And to get ahold of my captain and ask why Farelli was loose after the bust. *What had gone wrong during the shakedown?* But of course, he couldn't say that second part.

"And if you can't find the guilty person?" Her book lay forgotten in her lap. Apparently, his real-life soap opera was more interesting than Hemingway's characters and their drinking, arguing, and general discontent.

"Sucks for me," he retorted, sitting back in the chair. "Farelli will keep coming after me, and anyone I come in contact with. It would be in your best interest not to report me. Once he finds out about you…" He let the words trail off with a shake of his head. She shivered. Good girl, he thought. You can fill in the blanks on your own.

Rousing from the ugly picture he'd painted for her, she asked sharply, "So if it's that dangerous, why'd you go into the drug business in the first place? I mean, no one grows up saying they want to be a drug dealer."

He had to be careful. Not only was she attractive, she was smart.

"I can't tell you that," he replied in a serious tone. She started to shrug as if she expected nothing less from him, but then he concluded broadly, "Because then I'd have to kill you."

At her stunned expression, he chuckled. "Probably wasn't the best joke, was it? Sorry, Miss Parker."

The silence spun out. When she realized he wasn't going to answer the question, she abruptly rose from the couch. "I'd like to go to sleep, if that's all right with you." She began edging past him.

He stood and took hold of her arm. Gazed down into her immediately apprehensive face and felt her muscles tense within his grip. Once more he tamped down the urge to proclaim his innocence. "We're sleeping together. I want some shut-eye, and I need to know where you are. And that will be beside me. Any movement of the bed and I'll wake up. You can put a pillow between us if you must, but make no mistake—we *will* be sleeping in the same bed."

She yanked her arm from his grasp wordlessly. Gave no argument. After all, what was there to say? She was smart enough to know if she screamed and cried, ran or fought, they would only end up in another altercation where he would emerge the victor. As she moved to the bedroom listlessly, he saw her shoulders droop.

About-facing, he strode to the kitchen. He punished himself by washing the dishes, wiping the counters, doing the jobs he didn't like about cooking. Anything to stall going back to the bedroom. Part of him hoped little Miss Lucy Parker would be fast asleep by the time he entered the bedroom. Then he would be spared her accusatory glances. But part of him hoped she'd be awake. Because, for the first time in a long, long time, he was in the company of a person who wasn't out to get him.

With nothing more to keep him busy, he trudged down the hallway toward what would undoubtedly be another sleepless night. That old saying "no rest for the wicked" came to mind.

Giving a resigned sigh, he pushed open the bedroom door. Heard her breath catch. Her anxiety was a palpable thing, nearly as high as the mountain of pillows she'd constructed on top of the blanket.

He moved soundlessly through the dark room, eyes quickly adapting, and sat on the edge of the bed. It bounced as he shifted to find a comfortable position. The little squeak she made had him smirking humorlessly.

"Where'd you find all these blasted pillows, anyway?" he asked.

She said nothing, turning to face away from him.

He sighed. "So, it's going to be the silent treatment? Fine. It's been a long time since I've been on the receiving end of that form of argument. Sleep well, Miss Parker. Your virtue's safe with me." As the silence dragged on, and her nearness permeated his system, he felt it necessary to add, "But not because your body doesn't tempt me."

That comment had her shifting. A sound echoed over the pillow fortress between them, a mumbled, "Huh?"

Maybe she'd spoken the word, maybe he'd imagined it. "A Victoria's Secret model doesn't have anything over you. But I'm a man of my word, believe it or not. Good night."

At four in the morning, Jake jerked awake as if he'd set a timer, but it was just his internal alarm from years of discipline. He lay on his back for several minutes, listening to the sound of his bedmate's even breathing. At least she was sleeping now.

It had taken her over an hour to drift off. He knew, because it had taken him even longer, knowing she was worried about him next to her. That, and the fact he hadn't been this close to a woman in ages. His body kept strenuously reminding him of that fact. He regretted feeling Lucy Parker's soft curves during her escape attempt. He'd been in some form of arousal ever since then. Not that he'd ever act on it.

But even the feel of the heavy blankets resting on top of him had teased his hard-on to new heights. Once he had finally fallen asleep, he'd been plagued with sex dreams so vivid he'd jolted awake with one hand around his shaft. Thank God it was time for him to leave. Maybe a cold blast of pre-dawn morning air would alleviate this ridiculous sexual stupor.

Moving carefully so as not to disturb his companion, Jake slipped from the bed. Standing next to it, he eyed Lucy's shape. She lay on her side, facing away from him, and once more he felt the sting of remorse for treating her so vilely.

He wished they could have met earlier, although Lucy's nice-girl style probably would've set her firmly in the do-not-date category. His previous dates had been for one thing and one thing only. A good lay in between assignments. That's why he'd been able to rotate them out of his life quickly. Sure, there'd been times when he'd contemplated something more substantial, something lasting, but his occupation precluded that. Having seen what his mother went through each time his father disappeared for weeks at a clip, he wasn't about to ask any woman to wait around for him.

But now? Now, after he'd realized he no longer wanted this transient lifestyle, Lucy Parker fit all the criteria he'd once rejected. She screamed substance, in her mind and form, and he found himself grudgingly admiring that. She could think on her feet; she wasn't as scared of him as he would have liked, and that, dare he say, *sweetness*, made him want to sweep her up and hold her close. Shit, when was the last time he'd had a sentiment as sappy as that? But until he got his life back, there was no place in it for a sexy, glasses-clad girl in a Hello Kitty sweatshirt.

Turning to leave, he swung back around. Allowed himself one last brush with innocence. He reached out and pinched some of that long, rich brown hair between two fingers. And resisted the urge to raise it to his nose. Instead, he let it drop from his fingertips with regret. Shaking his head at his own fancifulness, he glided out of the bedroom.

First, he returned her car to working condition and then he replaced the battery in the other vehicle. After some false starts, the jeep's engine turned over, sparing him from adding insult to injury and stealing Lucy's car, though he had taken the cash from her wallet. Add theft to his growing list of offenses.

With a last glance at the cabin, he shifted the jeep into drive, and Jake Dalton began his journey back into the world he'd been forced to abandon.

Someone would pay for that.

Chapter Five

Lucy woke, body tensing as memory returned. Yesterday she'd been kidnapped and forced at knifepoint to drive an escaped convict to freedom. She'd been manhandled into submission. She'd broken bread with the criminal and been forced to sleep with him. What did she have to look forward to today?

Her breath hitched. He'd said things to her last night. Inappropriate things that had her thinking far into the night, while he'd kept to his promise and left her completely alone. She stared up at the indistinct ceiling and considered his ridiculous assertions regarding her looks. She wondered where he got the idea that she looked like a model. Especially a Victoria's Secret one.

Even so, she surreptitiously ran her hands down her sweatsuit clad body, feeling full breasts and the flare of ample hips under the barrier of clothing. She shook her head. The man was nuts and sex-starved. She'd never been mistaken for a model. Never had been, never would be.

Tossing his comments aside, she listened harder. Still nothing from his side of the bed. Carefully, she raised her head and stared over the mound of dividing pillows.

Her companion was gone.

She hopped into action after glancing around the room, sliding out from under the plaid bedclothes and rushing to the bedroom doorway. She pressed her ear to the gap to catch any sounds in the house. Silence.

Easing out between the door and the jamb, she tiptoed down the hall and headed into the living area, eyes darting everywhere, muscles clenched for flight. But only stillness crashed against her heightened senses. Maybe she really was alone. She rounded the doorway like a James Bond wannabe, peeking around the frame with one eyeball, back against the wall. The only accessory she lacked was a gun.

The kitchen was as empty as the rest of the rooms. Immediately, her eyes latched on to the kitchen window overlooking the carport. She moved to it and peered out.

There stood the Honda, hood down, waiting like a trusty steed.

Without thought, she swung the door open and careened down the steps to her car. Sliding inside it, she found the key still in the ignition where she'd forgotten it yesterday. She turned it on a prayer and grinned when the car sputtered to life, engine settling down into a reliable hum. The convict had replaced the car's parts. He'd kept his word. She was free to go.

Lucy grappled with the gearshift before throwing it into reverse. In moments, she roared down the dirt road, a rooster tail of dust chasing the car in its wild escape. Did she know where she was? Where she was going? It didn't matter. Anywhere besides where she'd been was an improvement.

Within minutes she'd returned to the main road, navigated blindly in the direction she thought she'd driven the day before. Had it been only yesterday? She felt as if a lifetime had passed since she'd embarked on her girls-only weekend.

Once on the paved road, heading for what she hoped was the highway, Lucy decided to call Jane, tell her she'd been kidnapped. And then realized the convict had kept her phone. She could have screamed her frustration. Why, oh why, couldn't this nightmare end?

She took a steadying breath. She was safe for the moment. Free. She'd stop off at the first sheriff's station she passed and report her kidnapping. She didn't buy his whole drug-lord excuse about drawing attention to herself. Of course he wouldn't want her to tell the authorities about her abduction. But she couldn't *not* say anything either. That would make her an accomplice in his escape. With her phone in his possession, the authorities could probably trace his whereabouts. The search for him still had to be going strong, even though she hadn't seen any evidence of that so far on the road.

When she finally passed a highway patrol insignia, she took the ramp and drove right to the building. The mountain station itself didn't engender confidence when she pulled in. It displayed architecture dating back to the seventies and the lot sported potholes and faded parking space lines. The only encouraging sign about the place was the parked patrol cars.

Good for her. She walked inside and immediately told the middle-aged officer at the desk that she'd been kidnapped by the escaped convict Nicky Costas. Just like that, she had the attention of every person in the room.

One of the officers, higher up in rank, she thought, broke from the group and approached her. He calmly asked if she needed a rape kit ordered. Embarrassed at the topic, she nevertheless negated the request. And remembered how often Costas had told her she was in no danger from him. She brought her mind back around to the moment at hand.

They began firing questions at her: when did he kidnap her, where did they go, what had he been wearing? While one officer wrote down her answers, another shoved a color mug shot under Lucy's nose, and she found herself staring down into an unsmiling, exact replica of Nicky "Jake" Costas.

As she gazed into his eyes in the photograph, she felt that same weird zing of attraction she'd had in person. That trip of her pulse and hitch in her breath. What was wrong with her? Being drawn to an escaped prisoner was even worse than supporting Jobless Bob for months on end. She really did have a double dose of her mother's gullibility when it came to men.

Or it was Stockholm Syndrome—finally her mind was firing on all cylinders and she could remember the name. Yes. That was it. There was a perfectly rational explanation for her misplaced feelings—they even had a name for the disorder.

She was *not* her mother.

Pushing the photo back toward the officer, she nodded. "That's him." The man who'd massaged her wrists. Who had cooked her dinner. Who had told her he found her so attractive—

Best not to think about what she'd felt against her

during that scuffle in the bathroom. It had just been a natural male reaction after weeks of captivity. As had been his words about her looks. She knew better than to fall for compliments from a desperate man.

At last she was free to go, exhausted from endless questions about her ordeal and filled to the brim from the bottomless cups of coffee offered to comfort her. She'd overheard muted phone conversations with the officials in charge of finding Costas, with his handlers from the prison. The station had suddenly become a beehive, and she was the cause of it. She couldn't help but wonder what it would all mean for Jake when they finally located him. How would he react when cornered by guns and cars and helicopters? Would he know it was because of her? He would have to. But, what if they shot him? Isn't that what happened when U.S. Marshals and local authorities conducted a manhunt?

Oh God.

As she walked out into the rutted parking lot, she swallowed the nasty bile that rose in her throat from the vision of her kidnapper cornered by all the chase vehicles like a scene from a Jason Bourne movie. She steeled herself against the immediate wash of pity. Just because he hadn't attacked her personally, had actually apologized for his behavior, that didn't negate the fact that he'd still kidnapped her with a weapon and held her against her will. She would have nightmares of the event.

Wouldn't she?

With the image of Jake stroking her battered wrists rising in her mind, she wondered. And questioned her actions. She'd reported her kidnapping against Jake's urgings and she'd asked to be kept out of the media circus that had already begun since Nicky Costas' escape. The police had said they'd be able to do that for now. But no matter how hard she tried to erase the past twenty-four hours from her mind, it had still happened. She was the proof.

She'd done the right thing. Hadn't she?

He'd made it. Three jacked cars later and countless to-go cups of coffee behind him and Jake Dalton had finally made it back to civilization.

Technically, he was parked down the street from Jerry's cover apartment. Going to his own would have been suicide. He had made some effort to change his appearance back at the cabin by shaving off his beard. Once in town, he'd visited the lower level of the public parking garage around the corner from his place. Before this case started, he'd stashed an emergency backpack filled with a change of clothes, two hundred dollars in small bills, and his favorite sidekick, a Beretta with a full clip, under the metal ramp leading to the wheelchair entrance. He'd learned over the years to be prepared.

Once bolstered with a weapon, a change of clothes, hastily-dyed auburn hair, and sunglasses, he'd tested his disguise by going into the local post office in search of a PO box Jerry had told him about ages ago, a safety net he'd called it. Jake hoped it would hold the answer to why Farelli was accusing him of stealing his money. But, like all his shitty luck lately, he'd found he couldn't just wiggle the lock free on the PO box. It would need more finessing and Jake didn't feel comfortable being out in the open too long. He'd decided to confront Jerry about it and then go from there.

The next order of business was calling his captain. It was a risk using Lucy Parker's cell phone, but he had to try. By now everyone knew of his escape the day before, so he wanted to check in and give his side of the story. And then he was going to pay Jerry a little visit and see who the hell had sent Farelli's goons sniffing around him.

Jake punched in the numbers of his captain's private line. While he waited for the connection, his gaze swept over the street from side to side as he'd been trained to do so many years ago. No delivery trucks, repair vans, or Caltrans vehicles lingered about the road, harboring undercover cops. Or worse.

"Who is this?"

Ah, yes. Captain Ralph Innes didn't mince words. Jake smiled slightly. Some things never changed. And then he got down to business.

"Cap'n, it's me. Dalton. If you ever respected me as a cop, let me talk before you send out the troops."

"Ah, hell, Jake. Why'd you run? You knew you'd get sprung before your trial. Now I've got a manhunt to try and control. Couldn't you have stayed where you were? It was your cover's only safety insurance."

Jake looked out the windshield at the near-empty street. Narrowed his eyes. "Yeah, well, seems like that insurance policy lapsed, Cap. Some friends of Farelli's paid me a visit while I was in the can. Wanted to know where his money was. Threatened to start hacking away some of my favorite body parts, beginning with my fingers, if I didn't give up its whereabouts. I like my fingers, boss, so what the hell is going on?"

Silence on the other end of the line met Jake's question. He knew his commanding officer. Innes was gauging just how much he wanted to divulge to his runaway operative. Jake couldn't fault him, even if the knowledge rankled. Many a cop had been swayed by the lure of confiscated goods and cash.

Finally a sigh let Jake know Innes was done thinking. For now. "That's what we want to know. Have you seen any unaccounted for cash lately?"

Jake felt the top of his head blow off at the accusation. "Are you shittin' me, Cap'n? Did you really just ask me if I've stolen evidence?"

Complete silence was the only response. Jake felt the noose of entrapment loop around his neck. Tighten imperceptibly.

"Listen to me, Dalton, before you go off half-cocked. We're missing money from that bust you were pulled in on—"

"And I'm the guy you automatically think of as the culprit? Jesus H. Christ, Cap. Think much of me?" It was time to wrap this reunion, Jake thought bitterly. No fatted calf for this prodigal son.

"Yeah, well, there've been accusations."

Oh, hell, this was just getting better and better. "By whom? The only person I worked close with was Jerry, and he wouldn't…"

The lack of agreement that met Jake's fading words spoke louder than a bullhorn. He began shaking his head.

"No, no, no. Jer wouldn't do that to me, Cap. Jerry's always had my back. He and I—"

"After we sprung him, Jerry said he saw you siphoning

some of the take before the bust. With his own eyes, Jake. I couldn't get your side because you ran." The sadness in the captain's voice told Jake his superior didn't want to believe it. "Why don't you come in? We'll talk about it."

"Screw that, boss. No more bars for me. You wanna talk, talk now. Better yet, you've said all I needed to know. That it's easier for my family, my home away from home, to believe I'm a traitor, a goddamn sell-out, than to overturn rocks and find the real culprit. I'll do this on my own. I'm getting used to working by myself, after all."

"I can't sanction that, Jake. You know better."

"Yeah, I know the drill. Your hands are tied. But mine sure as hell aren't." Jake made a restless move in the car. He needed to get on with his investigation, now that he was working alone.

"Just so you know. I had trouble believing Litton's story—"

"Don't smother me with kindness, boss. I don't think I can handle all the warm fuzzies I'm feeling right now."

"Shut up, Dalton."

Jake took the phone from his ear. Stared at it momentarily. His captain never talked like that. He replaced it. Innes was still speaking.

"…All that money we used in the sting? I had ours marked. By the serial numbers. Just like always. And some of it showed up at a gas station in Vegas, Jake. Just four days ago. Do you know what that means?"

Jake's mind raced. Yeah, he knew what the hell that meant. His pulse doubled at the implication. He spoke slowly, thoughtfully. "It means someone got greedy and skimmed before the bust. Took some of our evidence without knowing and spent it in Sin City. Who else knows about this?"

"No one. Yet. I buried the report, so I could hear your side of the story. But breaking out of lock up was the wrong move. You made yourself look bad, kid."

"So what's new?" Jake sneered at himself in the rearview mirror. He itched to end this confab. Wanted to confront his childhood buddy while he was unawares. He planned to wait for Jerry in his apartment, no matter how long it took for a reunion. It seemed they had a lot to talk about, and not just the mysterious PO box.

"Like I said, I can't approve what you've done. It's not department sanctioned. You'll be in hot water when we bring you in. So you might as well use your free time wisely. I would imagine the gas station outside Circus Circus has video cameras."

Once more Jake took the phone and stared at it. Had his captain just told him where the marked money had appeared? That, off the record, he wanted Jake to pursue leads? His spirits soared. His boss, his commander, still believed in him. And because of that, Jake was going to run with the ball. He had no choice. It was his life on the line, after all.

"I gotcha, Cap'n, loud and clear. I'll keep in touch."

Jake disconnected the call and stared unseeingly out the windshield once more. He swallowed the knot of disappointment that rose in his throat. Did their past mean that little to Jerry that he could accuse Jake of stealing evidence? Why? What mattered more to Jerry than their lifelong friendship?

Jake could only find out by confronting him.

Flipping Lucy Parker's blingy phone over, Jake began to field-strip it. Once he'd finished, he slid out of the driver's seat of the Datsun truck he'd hotwired at dawn, took the dismantled phone, and crushed it under his heel. Then he picked up the pieces and tossed them into the truck bed. No sense in leaving evidence around.

He zipped up his hoodie against the cool morning air and trudged toward the rear of the apartment building. Once hidden behind the structure, he pocketed his sunglasses and moved to the fire escape, swung up to the second floor hallway window, which hung partially open. So much for security. Shoving it up soundlessly, no mean feat considering the rust build-up on the casement, he dropped through the opening, landing silently on the threadbare hall carpet. He crouched, waiting.

Silence.

Not wasting any time, he moved down the hall, stopping off at the shared laundry room on this floor to pick up the apartment key he knew Jerry would have taped to the bottom of the folding table for safekeeping. It was something Jake did for extra precaution, as well. Palming the key, he headed toward his friend's unit, hoping no residents would pop out on their way to work. His luck held, and the key slid into the lock. The door latch clicked, and he was in.

He sighed as he pushed the entrance door shut and leaned against it, glancing around the dim space that mirrored his own shitty pad. Just enough crap out to look like someone lived there, but nothing incriminating or too personal.

Remaining where he was, Jake let his eyes tour the room. When they lit on dishes stacked by the sink, he made a mental fist pump. Jerry had been here, and recently. Maybe he still was.

Jake crept down the short hall toward the bedroom on

stealthy feet. As Nicky he'd only been here once or twice, but these places were all the same. He passed the bathroom, its door open. Reclining against the wall beside the only other door, which was ajar, Jake gripped the Beretta and silently counted to three.

So carefully that he didn't even disturb the air around him, he raised his free arm and pushed the door wider. And nearly jumped a foot when he heard a gun cock and a familiar voice say, "When I'd heard you escaped, I knew you'd come here, Jake. I've been waiting for you. Give me the gun, partner."

Partner.

Jake curled his lip at the title. When was the last time he'd had a partner, been a partner? It seemed like forever. He watched as Jerry rose and stood by the bed. Jake kept his gaze on his partner's arm and the steady aim of the Walther PPK with a suppressor pointed at his forehead. Jake maintained his own stance with arm extended and the Beretta unwaveringly fixed on Jerry's chest. They were at an impasse, but there was no way Jake was coming out the loser.

Hammering back, he said with a calm he was far from feeling, "Long time, no see, Jer. Done anything unusual lately? Like, oh, I dunno. Maybe stab your *partner* in the back?" Jake narrowed his eyes at the man he'd once claimed to be "closer than a brother" and watched that person squirm. But the moment of discomfort was fleeting.

He squashed his misplaced empathy. "Hand over the gun, Jerry. You always said I was a crazy bastard, and now I have nothing to lose." Wiggling the fingers on his free hand in a "c'mon" gesture, he watched the various emotions cross Jerry's face. His friend had always been easy to read. So how the hell had he managed to siphon money from a mobster?

A tense few seconds passed. Just when Jake thought he'd have to make good on his threat, Jerry loosened his hold and let the PPK dangle from his forefinger.

"You win, Jake."

In that instant, Jake saw his friend the way he used to be, contrite after a disagreement and eager to reestablish their status quo. But this wasn't some pissant argument over where to go for a drink. This was life or death.

"Of course I do, dickwad. I always do."

Motioning with the Beretta, he had Jerry precede him to the main room.

"I take it you checked in with the captain," Jerry said over his shoulder. "I knew you'd be sore, Jake. But I can explain."

"Explain what, Jer? That you chose to flush our twenty-year friendship down the toilet to join the other side?" Jerry turned when he got to the front room, and Jake glared at his well-dressed friend over the gun. Hardened his tone. "Look at you and me, Jerry, and use your detective skills. Which one of us would you suspect of stealing the evidence?"

"Shut up, Jake. You don't know anything. I did it for us—"

"Bullshit. Don't try to rationalize playing Judas. You changed sides for yourself and fingered me because you knew I'd act like a cop and nail your sorry ass."

"You should have stayed inside, Jake," his former partner snapped, voice cracking. "Listen to me, damn it."

Jake met his ex-partner's pleading expression and had a moment's doubt. He steeled himself against that weakness.

Moving carefully, he sat down in a ratty recliner while

still pointing the Beretta at Jerry, who shuffled back and forth nervously in front of him. He should be nervous. Of the two of them, Jake had always managed to be more conniving.

"I'm all ears." Jake hid the pain of his friend's betrayal under a sneer.

"Yes, I was skimming some of Farelli's take." At Jake's disappointed grunt, Jerry waved a hand. Jake subsided, studying his long-time buddy with a painful expression and knots in his stomach. He didn't think he would like what he was about to hear.

"All that money got to me," Jerry finally said. "Working with it day in, day out. Seeing what it could buy. I mean, let's face it, we were never going to get rich on our salaries. Our retirements would be living in shitholes like this one. So, I figured, why not supplement our incomes? Why should all that money go into evidence? Or, worse yet, back onto the streets? Up kids' noses. Skimming a little could make my life, *our* lives, so much better. We could buy that restaurant we planned." He leaned forward to emphasize his words. "No one needed to know how we got the money."

Jake's heart sank. His friend, his partner, really believed all the crap he was spewing. Oh, for Christ's sake…

"But I wasn't the only one skimming, Jake."

Jake started.

"You know I was one of the counters. That's how I was able to lift a little with no one finding out. But then, when we were tasked to recount each evening, Farelli's final take didn't add up with what I'd siphoned off. Someone was skimming after me." His voice had dropped to a whisper, as if just discussing his fraudulence would have Farelli materializing into their midst.

Though it didn't exonerate Jerry from his treachery, his explanation did coincide with their captain's comments. That another party was helping himself to the spoils. Jake returned to his friend's earlier statement. "So how does all this figure in to me being safer inside? Or you letting the captain think I was dirty? That shit doesn't make any sense."

"Because I can figure out who's behind it if I keep doing what I'm doing. I'm in the perfect position to do it as money counter. You weren't."

"You made sure of that, dickweed. Don't try to act like you're still on the case, Jerry. You just want deeper pockets. And, in the meantime, I remain everyone's favorite scapegoat—"

"That's right, Jake. For once in my life I'm going to be the guy to solve the case. All these years you've gotten the glory, jumped in front to take the spotlight. You were always being appointed lead detective, leaving me to take orders from you. But not this time, Jake. Not this time. This time I have the chance to be the man of the hour."

Jake gaped at his partner, couldn't believe the venom pouring from Jerry's mouth. Jealousy? Seriously? His friend had sold him out because he wanted to be the hero. And, um, newsflash—embezzling wasn't going to win Jerry any accolades.

That was when they both heard it. A slight ping. Nothing loud. Not a shatter or anything pronounced, but the pop of glass like the bounce of a marble, followed by the tearing sound of the cheap window shade. Their gazes met. The sudden recognition in Jerry's mirrored what Jake was feeling, and then a bloom of blood appeared in the center of Jerry's forehead. His eyes glazed.

Jake watched as his high school buddy and long-time partner, toppled to the floor at Jake's feet in slow motion, a sniper's bullet taking his life. Jesus, a fraction of a second and his friend was...gone.

He stared at the tiny, hole in Jerry's forehead. And then he heard another sound, much closer. A click and whine, like that of a detonator priming. Jerking his head toward the bedroom, Jake jumped to his feet. He lunged for the apartment's front door as his friend's home exploded in a firestorm of plaster, wood, metal, and glass.

Chapter Six

"... It's time to get up."

"Mmmmm, don't stop," Lucy sighed, stretching like a cat in the rumpled bed. Her lover's skillful hands stroked down her back, cupped her buttocks, and then skimmed on a return journey to her neck and shoulders, erotically kneading cramped muscles along the way. She couldn't suppress the moans of pleasure the massage elicited.

Her companion chuckled as he leaned over her from behind, lips tickling her earlobe and sending delicious shivers down her spine. He whispered seductively, "I don't want to, Pretty Kitty. But you have to go to work."

"Don' wanna," she purred, beginning to shift to her back. She hoped his expert fingers and mouth would do their magic on her front, would torture and tease her to that pinnacle that would spiral her into sexual orbit—

Wait. Had he just called her Pretty Kitty? Here, in her

bed? Only one person had used that nasty moniker. In growing disbelief she realized that the man who straddled her was none other than her kidnapper, Nicky "Jake" Costas. He grinned devilishly, warm hands anchored at her hips, starting to slide past their flare toward no man's land...

Her abductor was in *her* bed, sending her to pleasurable heights with just his touch? Those full, curved lips lowered inch by tantalizing inch toward hers, smiling a promise of illicit diversion while still not addressing her by her name—

"Lucy, wake up."

Lucy's eyes popped open. She blearily blinked away the image of Costas doing inexplicably delicious things to her body and found herself sprawled across her work desk. Jane stood in the opening of Lucy's cubicle. Holy moly, that dream had been too realistic...

She didn't know what was worse—getting caught sleeping on the job, or having said sleep contain erotic images involving a convicted criminal.

She hadn't slept well the last couple of nights. Restless thoughts kept her wakeful, as did shadows along the walls of her darkened bedroom. And now her kidnapper slipped into her subconscious, throwing her slumber into turmoil? He had no business invading her dreams or workplace in the form of naughty fantasies. God, how messed up was that?

So maybe she needed to heed the police chief's advice and seek counseling. This whole, um, *disorder*, where the victim fell in love with her captor—no. Nuh-uh. She most certainly was not in love. Or like. Or even "in lust" with an escaped convict. *You hear that, libido?* But obviously something wasn't quite right, because she couldn't erase Jake from her thoughts. She might banish him with some success during the day, but the moment she closed her eyes, he hijacked her subconscious. Stupid subconscious.

"You okay?" Jane stepped into Lucy's cubicle, a look of concern on her face. She was under the impression Lucy was recovering from the flu and that was why she hadn't made it to the weekend getaway. That was the excuse the convict had texted when he'd kidnapped Lucy. Not very original, but it had worked, and Lucy decided to stick with the story.

There was no way she wanted her coworkers knowing about her abduction. They gossiped more than high school students. And if they found out, she'd be forced to talk about the whole ordeal, the media would get wind, and her nice, quiet life would be gone. No, it was better this way. It was bad enough that the police said she would have to testify when Costas was caught. She wanted to enjoy her anonymity while she had it.

So Lucy shoved back her chair, and stood on wobbly legs. "Sorry. I haven't been sleeping well..."

Jane reached out to pat Lucy's shoulder. "I know, sweetie. The flu can be really nasty. You should have taken more time off. You get sick leave, you know."

Lucy met her friend's eyes, hoping her flushed face would resemble one freshly wakened from sickly slumber and not from the first throes of growing passion. How could she dream of that man? Did it mean she secretly lusted after him? Ewww. Although, if he hadn't been a kidnapper, a criminal, and an escaped convict. Well, yes, if he'd been just an average guy, even a Jobless Bob—yeah, okay, he would've been totally lust-worthy.

She tugged down her black sweater and pressed her hands over imaginary wrinkles in her black skirt. "I'm feeling better, Jane. Really." Forcing a smile, she changed the subject. "What did you come get me for?" She smoothed back her ponytail and adjusted her eyeglass frames, feigning nonchalance.

"They want the Stinson quarterlies, Luce. In Matheson's boardroom. Now."

Shaking off the images of the naked convict (how did she know what he looked like nude, anyway?), Lucy grabbed the required files off the stack on her desk and headed out the door, saying over her shoulder, "Thanks, Jane. Got 'em right here."

An hour later she had the Stinson taxes flagged as finished and ready to be sent out, with her boss pleased with her itemized work. His comment of, "I knew I could count on you, Parker," sent shivers down her spine. Was she so reliable that it was her name that came up when it was time to solve clients' tax dilemmas? She was the go-to girl?

The one who hooked up with the losers of the dating world, who secretly lusted after escaped prisoners, and who accepted praise from balding middle-aged businessmen to satisfy her need for conformity? Just what type of person had she become?

A scared one, Lucy thought as she threw herself into her desk chair.

Since the carjacking, she'd been on edge, jumping at loud noises and obsessively checking and rechecking all her locks. She fell asleep with her bedroom light on, but not until she'd laid awake until the wee hours, reliving the time she'd spent in Jake, no, *Nicky* Costas' company. Wondering what she could have done differently.

What she didn't understand was, if she was so scared of

him, why did he show up all naked and tanned (*tanned?*) in her dreams? Why did the idea of him in her bed send tingles through her body and heat between her thighs? What kind of woman was she, to lust after someone who'd taken her hostage…even if he'd been the handsomest man she'd ever met?

Casting her eyes about the cubicle so she didn't have to answer that question, her eyes lit upon a post-it note stuck to the frame of her computer monitor. In Jane's neat handwriting, it proclaimed, "Call your mom." She groaned. Just what she needed. A conversation with the older, drunker version of herself. She should never have given that woman her work phone number.

She knew when her mother phoned it would be an hour or more of whining on the maternal end of the line. Or, Lucy could suck it up and go on over and visit her pathetic parent. Then she would have fulfilled her daughterly duty for the month. Not that it ever mattered to that woman. She only looked forward to another sleepover with Tennessee's finest. Lucy grabbed her purse and slammed out of her cubicle. She wouldn't be returning to work afterwards.

She'd escaped a neglected childhood, dodged another dead end relationship, and survived a kidnapping. Why couldn't she escape the guilt this upcoming meeting guaranteed?

Forty minutes after her reunion with Mommy Dearest, Lucy parked in her apartment carport. And sat a moment while the engine ticked comfortably around her.

The visit with her mother had gone pretty much like she'd thought it would: the older woman begged for money while Lucy swallowed the pity she always felt when she saw her mother swaying on her feet, drunk since shortly after noon.

Naturally, she'd given in. Paid the landlord for her mother. She certainly didn't want the woman forced to live with her—which didn't sound very daughterly, but her mom could be vicious. As an adult, she chose to avoid the verbal and emotional abuse.

As it was, when she hadn't given her mom "enough" cash, she'd been forced to weather the shouts and accusations of being a heartless daughter. She still wasn't immune to the nasty name-calling, though she'd danced this dance all her life. A childish part of her would always love her mother. And it was that love that won out over the "cut your losses" attitude of her grown-up self.

With the reunion over for this month, Lucy heaved a sigh of relief. Getting out of her car, she headed for the apartment that was an oasis in her solitary life. The complex she lived in wasn't new, but with age came mature vegetation and older neighbors, both facets she liked. Today, especially, she felt the problems of earlier drop away from her shoulders as she moved along the winding sidewalk to her third floor home.

The leaves of the eucalyptus trees surrounding the building rustled in the autumn evening breeze. Weak pathway lighting illuminated her way, but the stairs remained shadowed. The automatic porch light hadn't come on yet. Lucy continued confidently forward. Her home had always been her sanctuary, private and secluded the way she liked it. Trotting up the stairs to her door, fumbling for the key in her purse, she nearly missed a step when she spied a dark shape huddled in the alcove off her front door.

Fear clawed its way up her throat, an instant spew of panic ready to become a scream. She was catapulted back into that first moment of shock when the runaway prisoner leaped into her car. Clutching the railing, she turned to flee, terror driving her like a hound nipping at her heels.

"Wait!"

She faltered in her headlong rush, head jerking around as she recognized the voice with just that one plea. And the porch light chose that moment to flicker on, illuminating the speaker and confirming her worst suspicions. It was her kidnapper, Nicky Costas, aka "Jake." Lucy almost fainted at the realization.

What was he doing here? How had he found her? Scrabbling once more in her purse, she remembered too late that he still had her phone. She couldn't call 911. As comprehension dawned, she also noticed something about Costas. He looked like he'd been in some kind of explosion. His face had streaks of blood and dirt. His clothes were covered in dust and plaster, as was his now reddish hair.

Lucy cocked her head. Even from this distance she could see the glassy sheen in his eyes. The wide, vacant stare. He was in shock, like a car accident victim. He began to rise, struggled to his feet like he was injured, and right away she swung around to bolt. But not before she saw him sway wildly and begin to topple toward her.

Automatically, she shot out an arm and caught him around the waist before he tumbled past her. She could feel tremors jittering through him, as if he'd been in the snow without a jacket. Then she looked into his face, so close to hers. Big mistake.

"I'm so sorry," he whispered. "I had nowhere else to go."

They were near enough she could see the individual scratch marks on his cheeks and across his nose. The blood had dried and the dirt had smeared.

"What happened to you? How did you find me?" She shifted her stance to better support his solid frame. He tried to straighten and relieve her of some of his weight. One of her hands moved to the center of his chest as support, for him or for her she didn't know. The warmth of his body seeped through the sweatshirt and unfamiliar clothes he wore, but he continued quaking from within.

"I...um...looked at your driver's license when I borrowed your cash." He pulled out of her arms, but they still stood close beneath the lamplight. The feeble glare from above glinted off the dull red highlights in his hair, a red she didn't remember from their earlier acquaintance.

"Yes, thanks for leaving me with nothing. And, that explains how, but not why. Or what happened to you." She held her ground, knew she could push him right down the stairs if he tried anything. Yet she also knew he wouldn't. Jake had been many things, but he'd never been abusive.

He inhaled a deep breath and let it out on a shudder. Then met her look head on. "I won't hurt you, I promise. I can explain everything, if you'll just take me inside with you. Let me stop running for a while." His look was pleading, his words sincere. She hesitated. He was an escaped drug dealer, after all.

But, like she'd concluded just a moment ago, he'd already had the chance to rape her. To kill her and bury her on that mountaintop. And he hadn't. However, she still stalled.

"There's a Motel 6 just down the road," she said. "You have money. *My* money." She moved aside to put space between them. He radiated so much heat, and her body seemed to absorb it all.

He bit off a curse, ran a shaking hand through his tangled hair. "I used that already for gas. It wasn't a whole hell of a lot. And then I was too busy escaping the explosion of my partner's apartment—after he was shot in the forehead by a sniper's bullet."

Lucy gaped at him while his statement sank in. Which shocked her more: his calmly stated comment about a sniper's bullet or the fact that he'd used the word *partner*?

"Since when do drug dealer's work with partners? And if you're in such a dangerous position, why would you bring it all to my doorstep? I like my home. I don't want it blown up!" She could hear the hysteria in her voice, and she wished she could control the bubble of fear as it gathered within her.

It was his turn to reach out, grasp her elbow. Immediately she yanked free.

"I'm not a drug dealer. I'm a cop. An undercover cop. Please, I can prove who I am if you'll just give me the chance. Let me inside. We're sitting ducks out here in the open."

Lucy cast her eyes about at his last words. She searched the shadows. Was that a man under the stairs across the way? Or was it an overgrown bush? She looked back at the convict. For the first time, she didn't feel safe in her apartment community. And he was to blame.

Costas held up his hands in supplication. "I promise, after I've given you proof of who I really am, if you still don't believe me, I'll leave without any argument. It's just safer if we talk inside."

Lucy stared at him, conflicted. He'd kept his word the last time, but that was no guarantee. Or was it? She'd been totally at his mercy then. Here at least she had the home court advantage. Neighbors that would hear her if she screamed.

Making up her mind, Lucy pulled out her key and edged around him. She unlocked the front door with a quick flick of her wrist. Waved a hand for him to precede her.

"Company first."

The look he flashed her before he stepped inside hid humor in its depths, and she felt the knot within her ease ever so slightly. A man intent on committing violence wouldn't appreciate her sarcasm. She hoped.

Once inside she flicked on the living room light, twisted the knob lock until it clicked, and considered whether or not to flip the deadbolt. Keeping crazy killers out or trapping oneself inside with one…hmm. Tough call.

When he moved past her, limping with shoulders hunched, she opted to bolt the door. Then she dropped her purse on the edge of the couch under the front window and automatically toed off her pumps.

She paused and took the moment to study him and really take in his appearance. In addition to the scrapes and smudges on his face and the debris caught in his hair, his clothes sported rips and tears. It was evident he'd been in some kind of recent altercation.

His brown eyes had lost some of their vacancy. Only an occasional tremor seemed to pass through him now. While she studied Costas, he was busy examining his surroundings, taking in the green-patterned couch under the front window with its closed vertical blinds. He glanced over the light-colored laminate flooring into the shadowed dining and kitchen area, and then returned his gaze to the sofa.

Looking back at her he jutted his chin toward the seat and asked, "May I?"

Surprised at his unexpected courtesy, she took in his filthy attire and shook her head. "Not as dirty as you are. Now, start talking." She crossed her arms under her breasts and narrowed her eyes. Casting one more look of longing at her couch, he wiped a hand over his face. A smear of blood appeared on his cheek. Apparently one of his cuts was still oozing. She decided his explanation could be postponed.

"You're bleeding. Follow me." She stepped around him and headed toward the bathroom. Doubt about whether she was doing the right thing by believing him lessened every second she was in his company. Unlike in their first meeting, tonight Nicky Costas acted lost. Vulnerable, even. And that fact made her bleeding heart beat faster.

Flipping on lights as she went, Lucy pointed to the closed toilet in the bathroom. "Sit." Surprisingly, he did as he was told.

Although Jobless Bob had lived with her, making her no stranger to a male presence in the little apartment, Costas still seemed to take up more room in the small space than his size warranted. He dwarfed the vinyl fish swimming on the shower curtain and loomed in his corner of the bathroom.

Yet his submissive behavior continued as she brought out cotton balls and antiseptic from the medicine cabinet. Until he pulled a small, snub-nosed gun from the back of his pants and placed it on the bathroom counter. She stared at it as if it were a snake he'd deposited there. At last he cleared his throat and brought her attention back to him.

"It's to protect us, not to use on you," he said simply. She blinked and tried not to look at it while she resumed her activity.

"You can talk while I clean you up," she suggested. All of a sudden, she felt self-conscious in the tiny room, with her hands poised to dab at his abrasions and her breasts practically in his face. The moment seemed too intimate. She tried to ease back and felt her face flame when his gaze dropped to her chest.

His lashes were long and dark, thick crescents that shielded his eyes from hers as they remained downcast. More roughly than she'd planned, Lucy touched the first cheek wound with antiseptic and heard his hiss. She muttered a "sorry," before repeating the action. His back straightened, and she found him looking up at her once more.

"Jerry and I had infiltrated a drug operation in San Bernardino," he began quietly, and Lucy picked up a clean cotton ball, drenched it with medication, and moved to a cut near his hairline. This time she dabbed gently, and he didn't move. Brushing back some reddish strands to better see the wound, she found his hair soft and touchable.

"He worked in the money-end of the business, counting each drug take, while I delivered the goods, and sometimes filled in as one of Anton Farelli's bodyguards. We'd been working the sting for several months because we wanted enough evidence to actually bring in Farelli and make the charges stick. He'd always managed to slip through the legal system up to now."

His eyes drifted closed at this point, and Lucy realized with horror that she'd been smoothing his hair off his forehead over and over while he talked, caressing him as a lover might. But it felt so silky, so smooth…

She dropped her hands to her sides for a moment, and his eyes opened. She had trouble meeting them as they bored into hers with desire. Her knees began to tremble from the intensity of his gaze. She struggled to lock them, to continue with her care in a more matter-of-fact manner. But she couldn't control the gush of warmth pooling in her lower regions. She could only wonder at her untimely reaction.

He looked away, toward the colorful, fishy curtain. "When our captain thought we had enough evidence, the operation was raided and everyone was thrown in jail. Some of us were moved to state prison to await trials. We maintained our covers and knew within a few days we'd be released. Before I was sprung, however, I was visited by some hard-time goons on Farelli's payroll."

Lucy nodded. She remembered him telling her that back at the cabin. Only then he'd been Nicky Costas, drug dealer.

His hands moved to the top of his shirt. He undid a button, then another. And another.

She gasped.

His eyes widened, but he didn't stop until his shirt was nearly completely open. He tugged the fabric aside, revealing a mottled collection of bruises along his abdomen and chest. Lucy caught herself reaching toward his chiseled torso and stopped herself. She stared past the impressive muscles and defined abs, noting the yellowish and faded blue bruises marring his perfect skin.

"W-what's your real name?" she blurted, returning to her ministrations, focusing on his face.

He drew his shirt closed. "Jake. Jake Nicholas Dalton."

She looked at him, nodded, and then looked back at the last cut. With gentle fingers, she pressed under his chin. Lifted it slightly. He started talking some more, his warm breath wafting over her hands, creating goose bumps up her arms.

"Anyway, you know that part of the story. After I left you, I called my captain. Sorry about keeping your phone, by the way. But I needed it, though I had to destroy it afterwards so I wouldn't be traced." She looked into his eyes. "I *am* sorry. Anyway," he continued, "my captain told me Jerry, *my best friend Jerry*, fingered me as the one skimming the evidence money. Then Cap asked me to come in so we could talk about it. I declined. Before I hung up, he told me that some of the marked money showed up in Vegas *after* the bust."

"But you were in jail." His story was becoming a mental Rubik's cube. And then there was that unasked-for attraction she was feeling. With his face cleaned up and his hair neatly smoothed back—*don't go there!*—he was quite handsome.

"Exactly." Jake had warmed to his tale. Or he was nearing its end, for he kept talking while Lucy fought his magnetic pull. "Someone else was siphoning. So, since I was wanted by Farelli as Nicky, and wanted by my department as Jake, I paid Jerry a visit. And found him waiting for me. Pointing a gun in my face."

She blinked.

"That was my reaction. Seems ol' Jer was jealous of me solving our cases. He decided to throw doubt on me and get the glory by cracking this one. And, of course, he was skimming money too, but that's beside the point. Then someone shot him in the forehead and blew up his place."

Even though he'd already told her this part, she still

sucked in another breath. She couldn't imagine witnessing such a horrific event, let alone talking about it so calmly. Maybe he was in shock. When she'd recounted her abduction to the police, she'd done it in a level, monotone voice. She'd held it together remarkably well. Her relief at surviving and escaping murder/rape/mayhem had buoyed her spirits. Then, once she'd relayed her tale and made it home, she'd had a meltdown of epic proportions. But Jake didn't look relieved or calm or even on the brink of some cathartic crackup. He looked…defeated.

Something swelled in her chest and caused her eyes to water.

She bit her lower lip. She was *not* going to fall for another hard-luck story given by a good-looking man. The new and improved Lucy Parker learned from her mistakes. *But he looks so vulnerable…*

She took a deep, steadying breath. "So, if I believe you, and that's a big *if*, what happens next? If you're wanted by both sides of the law, what are you going to do now?"

They stared at each other in the brightly-lit bathroom. He held her gaze.

"Next? Next, hopefully I prove to you that I'm one of the good guys, and you let me stay here so I can get back on the case. I have a few leads involving Jerry that I need to check out. A PO box he told me about ages ago that might rustle up some threads to follow, for one. I was going to confront him about it at his apartment, but he was killed before I could."

Her gaze shifted to his reflection in the mirror. The silence in the small room was absolute while she considered his words and felt her resolve weakening. At some point during their reunion her initial fear at his reappearance had dissipated, replaced by curiosity. Curiosity about whether he was exactly who he said he was: a cop.

She met his eyes in the mirror, squared her shoulders. "How are you going to prove to me you are what you say you are?"

"Do you have a computer?"

Chapter Seven

"He's holed up in an apartment in East Palm Court, Mr. Delano."

"That's not where he lives." Michael frowned, pacing the budget motel's thin carpet with his phone to his ear, trying to make sense of the story his gofer was reporting.

After successfully "making a statement" by taking out that stupid schmuck Tommy—a very satisfactory moment—he'd hoped to get rid of Nicky Costas in the subsequent blast. It wasn't what Farelli had wanted, but putting down both those troublemakers would have gotten rid of a lot of head aches as far as Michael was concerned. He could weather whatever storm Farelli dished out. But he couldn't withstand an investigation into the missing money.

"No sir, it's not. And it was too dark to see who let him in. Looked like a girl, though."

Michael paused in his pacing. A girl? This was a promising development. He hadn't thought Costas had a piece of tail on the side, had even thought he might swing the other way, the way he schmoozed with all the guys. But having a girl opened up options for Michael. A man was always weakest when the woman he was banging was threatened. He made up his mind.

"Take some pictures, but for Chrissake don't get noticed. I don't want him aware he's under surveillance. And give me the address. If anyone is going to approach him, it'll be me."

After cutting the connection, Michael tapped the phone against his chin, deep in thought. He needed to make a move soon. Whether he put the lid on Jake's can of worms or not, Farelli would be more vigilant from now on. And that meant it was pretty much the end of the gravy train for him. It wasn't like he didn't have a contingency plan set up for just this sort of occurrence. Airline ticket, an offshore account. A new identity. But it rankled that he would have to walk away.

Those two flatfoots should have stuck to writing traffic tickets.

"Have a seat. I can prove who I am."

An hour after Lucy agreed to let him stay the night, Jake was finally going to verify his true identity.

First, she'd let him shower and rinse away the reminders of Jerry's death. He still couldn't erase that horrifying moment when the tiny hole appeared in Jerry's forehead. That, and Jerry's betrayal, he knew, would stay with him for the rest of his life.

Lucy had taken his dirty clothes after providing him with some clean ones she'd said had been left behind by her "ex."

That word had given him pause, but he couldn't explain why.

"You've been married?" he'd asked her as she ducked into her walk-in closet. He tried to wrap his brain around that eventuality, but he couldn't. Once married to the woman in front of him, who in their right mind would leave her? She was pin-up model perfect as far as he was concerned, with all those round curves he still remembered from their tussle at the mountain cabin. Add in those sexy-adorable glasses that made her huge eyes even bigger and all that long, dark hair, he was in danger of forgetting the reason he was here in the first place.

But it wasn't just her looks that he admired. No, it was also her mind and, holy shit, he'd never thought he'd be praising a woman for her quick wit. He'd observed back at the cabin how she analyzed anything tossed her way. How, though he'd scared her shitless with that shiv and bastard routine of his, she'd stood up to him. Challenged him.

And now, when he showed up at her home, she'd allowed him inside, had even tended to his wounds with his weapon resting beside her pretty little dish of fancy soap. She hadn't gone all hysterical. Rather, he'd seen the wheels circling in that logical brain of hers while he'd talked, turning over his words to ferret out the truth.

He admired that ability, especially since he went with his gut so much of the time. Found it the ultimate turn-on, actually. No, Lucy was a woman you could sink your teeth into, physically and metaphorically. One who could tease your dick and your brain. Her ex must have been a schmuck.

Her answer to his question had been a laugh and an, "Oh, pleeaassse, don't insult me. I wouldn't marry any of the losers I've been with."

Unexplainable relief had flowed through him. He really needed to dial down his growing attraction. It wouldn't do for him to act like a poodle with a fuzzy slipper around her. This girl deserved more.

Now he patted the couch seat beside him and tried not to notice how, instead of her latest sweatshirt's bulky material turning him off, he wanted to reach out and smooth his hand over all that pink softness. He shifted to relieve the sudden tightness in his pants and cleared his throat.

"When cops go undercover their real lives are wiped out, right down to the tiniest details on the internet, but I found an article from years ago in the local paper when I graduated from the academy. A bit blurry, but you can still make me out. Lemme bring it up." He looked down at the laptop screen, relieved to have someplace else to focus upon. His fingers took command of the keyboard.

"Here." He turned the computer toward her and she leaned forward, squinting at the screen where he'd brought up an indistinct class picture of squeaky-clean cadets. His graduating class. "Look at the number of people in the row, and then look at the number of names," he instructed. "My name was cut out, and so was Jerry's, but you can see us clear enough in the middle of the group. And if this isn't enough proof, hell, go Google the rest of the names to see if they line up with the other guys in the class." He sat back on the couch while she pulled the computer onto her lap and studied the group shot.

He knew when she found him. She leaned into the screen, like a pointer who'd caught the scent. He looked over her shoulder to see what she saw. He'd been incredibly young back then, his hair buzzed short. Thank God he didn't have to wear that haircut anymore.

And then he frowned as he took in the other fresh-faced young man grinning back at the camera. The one who'd slung an arm around Jake's shoulder. The one who had dropped like a stone at his feet this very afternoon, dead at thirty-three.

"How old were you?" she asked quietly. His attention had been so riveted, he wondered if she'd asked the question more than once. He shook his head to clear it.

"Twenty-one. Thought I knew everything. No bad guy was too bad for me. I'd make the world a better place to live, one criminal at a time. Me and Jer, nothing was gonna stop us." He paused as the past bombarded him. "But a bullet stopped Jerry, didn't it? Right between the eyes." He pointed a finger gun at the computer. "*Pop* and there was the hole. Just one little hole that wiped out everything we'd planned. Shit."

He stood abruptly and paced across the room, fists clenched. Stood with his back to her, fighting the tears threatening to overflow. God, he missed the jackass!

"A wasted life, all because of greed," he croaked. "Greed and impatience. 'We'll never make that kind of money' Jerry said to me before he died. 'Why should it all go back into evidence? They'll never miss it, and we could buy us that restaurant.'" Jake closed his mouth abruptly. The memories were too vivid. Even though Jerry hadn't finished his "someday we'll make it" spiel, Jake could imagine what his friend would have said next. Could almost hear his friend's scratchy voice as he'd say, "You could cook and I'll be the front room man. Can't you see it?"

He paced side to side. Couldn't bring himself to look at

Lucy. His emotions were still too near the surface. "We were *this* close to bringing Farelli down, and Jerry couldn't wait one more frickin' year. We would've brought down Farelli and then taken our early retirement together. Opened Jake and Jerry's Grill. No, he had other, bigger ideas, and now I'm hiding out from a sniper, with the mob on my back, with no one to trust—"

"You can trust me."

Jake blinked back into the present to find Lucy standing by the couch, listening to his rant and promising her allegiance. He'd momentarily forgotten all about her. And wondered how he ever could have.

Meeting her eyes behind those glasses, he wanted to tell her *no*. That he wasn't worthy of her trust. He was his father's son, after all. A person who could take something fine and turn it into shit. Hadn't he been the one to talk Jerry into going to the academy with him? To trust him? Look where that landed his friend. A hole in the head because he hadn't been strong enough to resist temptation. Hadn't Jerry always been weaker? A follower? Jake should have known that about him.

And now Lucy wanted to back him? He couldn't let her. One messed up life on his conscience was enough. Like hell if he'd take down Lucy, too. Intent on sending her running to her bedroom, Jake strode back to Lucy, invaded her space and glared into her upturned face. *Go away, little girl. Go away*, he chanted silently.

She didn't read his mind, damn her anyway. She held her ground and repeated quietly, "You can trust me."

He said nothing. Their combined breathing was the only sound in the room until Lucy nervously licked her lips. He stared hungrily at her mouth as she said softly, "For what it's worth, I'm sorry about your friend."

Ah, shit. She wasn't going to take the hint? She didn't see the danger of being with him, as a man or as a fugitive? That even though he'd taken pains tonight to show her he was one of the protect-and-serve types, he still was nowhere near worthy enough for a sweet and sassy girl like her?

Then to hell with his good intentions. He was going to take what she didn't even know she was offering.

"How sorry?" he rasped. "Sorry enough for this?" He swooped down to capture her lips.

Her mouth startled open, moist and inviting. She made this tiny, husky little moan and he was a goner. He nibbled, licked, teased with his tongue, and still he couldn't get enough. She drove him nuts, the fragrance of her hair, the soap she showered with. That wholly feminine scent that urged him to dominate her in the most primal of ways. He brought shaking hands up to anchor her head for his onslaught.

Words escaped his lips between bruising kisses, dirty words that he couldn't hold back any more than he could stop his assault on her mouth. And when, instead of shoving him away, she wrapped her arms around his neck and plastered her soft, pliant body against his, he knew one kiss wouldn't be enough.

His hands streaked up under her sweatshirt. He cupped her breasts, running his thumbs over her already tightened nipples encased in lace. Not satisfied, he plunged his hands inside those baggy sweatpants to grip that rounded ass that had tantalized him since her aborted escape out the cabin bathroom window. He ground his erection against her, never letting go of that heavenly posterior even as he crashed his mouth once more against hers.

Her eyes startled open when she felt his hardness. He knew, because he'd kept his own open, determined not to miss a flicker of emotion across her beautiful, expressive face. She hesitated. Pulled back slightly. She must have sensed the danger lurking in the depths of his roiling emotions.

Lifting his head a fraction, he squeezed her behind encouragingly. But the moment of abandon had passed. Slowly her hands dropped from the nape of his neck, burning over his shoulders and down his chest as she pressed her palms against his wildly beating heart.

Reluctantly, he let go of her ass, pulled his hands out of her pants. Jesus, he really was worthy of an eight-by-ten cage.

She backed away in edgy silence, shaking her head while turning and disappearing behind her bedroom door. He stared after her, berating himself for being ten times the fool. She'd allowed him to stay in her home, accepted his explanations as truth, and he'd thanked her by pawing her like a sex-starved teenager. He should have behaved better. He was the more experienced one, after all. The professional.

Ha, the only thing he was professional at was screwing up his life. And now he'd attempted to start on hers. Lucy didn't need a fugitive cop coming on to her. Lucy needed to know she was safe from the bad people in the world, and from him. He was doing a piss-poor job at assuring her of both of those things right now.

Jake swung away from the closed bedroom door and threw himself on the couch, glaring at the sleeping laptop screen, disgusted with the whole situation.

With the evidence of a past live-in man covering his ass, so to speak, Jake knew little Miss Hot Pants Parker wasn't a stranger to sex. But maybe her heart had to be actively involved. Most women had to imagine themselves in love, he had found, before they gave their bodies to a man. And what a body she could give, with those full breasts and that plump, heart-shaped ass a man could really grab ahold of...

This type of thinking was only going to guarantee him a sleepless night. Though the two of them might be mutually interested in each other, he remained a hot mess. He couldn't thrust his brand of turmoil onto Lucy. She deserved better. And they both knew it.

Jake reached for the laptop and dragged it to rest upon his knees. He shoved Lucy-of-the-tempting-body out of his mind, instead focusing on what his captain had told him earlier. That money had shown up in Vegas, at a gas station. He couldn't access that information online. But he could see who in Farelli's operation stood the best chance of being a thief.

He tried Jerry's bean counter colleagues first. Once again, he wouldn't go the official route. If he used his authorized login, his department, namely his captain, would be alerted to his activities and whereabouts through his IP address. Though Innes had told him to use his freedom wisely, Jake still didn't need his whereabouts becoming common knowledge.

No, he would have to Google each individual and see what public information he could dig up. It would be painstakingly slow, but hell, his first choice for how to spend the night was sure as shit not going to happen. On with the search.

About three hours later, Jake sat back on the couch and rubbed his eyes with the heels of his hands. Hell, he was exhausted. He'd certainly had a marathon day and night, something he didn't want to think about. Late night ruminations only guaranteed more sleeplessness.

As did what he'd discovered during his search. He'd been able to toss aside most of Farelli's underlings. Their bios read like an Average Joe's. Facebook, Twitter, Pinterest, you name it, they had the typical accounts. Not that many of them were posting to Instagram or tweeting. But their rap sheets from the public county records and insight into their families' social networking accounts—the wives and kids and mistresses—that's where he found a wealth of information. They looked like normal people with normal hobbies and pastimes, which was probably why Farelli hired them. They wouldn't stand out in a police investigation.

Until he got to Michael Delano, whom he'd considered a dick the moment he'd laid eyes on him. The man's public bio read like everyone else's. He lived in an average house in an average neighborhood of San Bernardino. He'd attended a local college, but didn't appear to have graduated. He'd had a few run-ins with the law that Jake couldn't investigate unless he wanted to advertise his whereabouts online. It was all too perfect. Delano worked for a drug lord, yet his history practically read like a Boy Scout's.

Was it the fact that he knew Farelli was a drug lord that made him suspicious? Or was it because he didn't like Delano? Probably yes on both counts. On a hunch, he keyed in his own name. Or, rather, Nicky's. He read the official crap the techno nerds at the station had manufactured for Nicky Costas. Then he clicked back to Delano's info. Read it again.

They read the same. Two different people, two different lifestyles, yet they read similarly. Blah histories, boring job backgrounds, brushes with the law, no family… No red flags. Not even any social media. Of course, looking at Delano as he knew him, Jake didn't think the man would have many cyber friends even if he did have accounts on the various social sites. The man screamed bad guy as if it was branded on his forehead.

Jake closed the laptop with a snap and stared at the bedroom door without seeing it. Instead, he saw all the words he'd been reading about the other Farelli employees, Delano, and lastly, himself. They swam in front of him like some weird kaleidoscope of letters. He half expected Vanna White to appear to put them in order.

And then they organized, settled into their respective patterns, and his pulse kicked up a notch. Delano's bio still read just as seamlessly as Nicky's, almost like it had been manufactured. Manufactured by techno nerds. Techno nerds that worked for a United States law enforcement agency.

Chapter Eight

Lucy sat in traffic the following evening, content to trail the car in front of her at the snail's pace it maintained. She had no desire to hurry home. Waiting there was a person she did not want to face.

After all, what did you say to a man you'd allowed to stick his tongue down your throat, as well as grope your body? A man you barely knew? "Oh, hey, you've got a talented tongue and expert fingers. Pass the salt, please."

Add to that the fact she knew she'd been on the verge of dragging him to her bed and she wished she could just keep driving, right on past her little place of tranquility and charm. But that wouldn't solve anything.

She'd managed to sneak out of the apartment this morning without waking him. That had been a stroke of luck. Unless, of course, he'd pretended to be asleep, all stretched out and boneless as he'd been. All rumpled and sexy, angelic, even, as he slept. Gah. *Stockholm. Stockholm. Stockholm.*

Okay, so she wasn't a captive. And he was a—presumably—innocent man on the run. A man with wicked good looks and an incredibly talented tongue.

She blew out a breath and focused on driving.

"Oh, God, what have I done?" She swung into the carport, wanting to find a hole and crawl into it. Last night she'd turned him on and off like a light switch, so how was she supposed to behave today? How was she supposed to ignore that she had practically thrown herself at him and then changed her mind?

Realizing all these thoughts were only giving her a headache, on top of the one she'd been sporting all afternoon, she flung herself out of her car and headed for her building. Just walking under the trees in the twilight lessened her anxiety by a few degrees. This is why she stayed here, and not in some modern townhouse. The peacefulness permeated her very being, relaxed her—

"Excuse me. Do you live here?"

Lucy's back stiffened as she turned toward the male approaching her from the right. Immediately, she ran a hand into her giant purse, fingers curving around the mace can that she now carried after her kidnapping by the very person waiting for her in her apartment. The one whose hands had burned her skin wherever he'd touched her…

"Yes," she replied automatically, blocking last night's erotic images from her mind. "May I help you?" She went instantly on guard when she faced the speaker.

Probably just under six feet, this stranger was *buff*. The camp-style, tan shirt he wore accented muscular arms and a flat stomach, as did the snug cargo pants over strong legs. Short, sandy brown hair, eyes she couldn't quite discern the color of in the dim light, and an engaging smile rounded out his appearance.

He stopped before her, eyes roving over what she knew was her messy ponytail, smudged glasses, chewed-off lipstick, and ink-spotted blouse, and smiled that megawatt smile again. "I'm sorry to bother you, miss, but I'm trying to find my Nanna's apartment. I've only been here once before and that was a long time ago. I've been working overseas, and now I can't remember where hers is. Frankly, this complex's layout is confusing. Can you help me?"

He held out a piece of paper while Lucy stared at him, her mind seeming to take forever to evaluate what he had asked. "Um, yeah, I can try. This place was built in the eighties, and then they added on, so it's like a maze. What's her number?"

The man handed the paper to her and she read what was written on it. She recognized the name and address. It was just two buildings to the right of hers.

"Now that I'm back stateside," he continued, "I'll be checking on her regularly. I worry about her living alone. Is there much crime here?"

Once more she met his unusually hypnotic eyes.

"Not that I know of. There are plenty of elderly renters, and they seem content. It's very safe here in East Palm Court."

"Good, that's good." He pointed to the address she still held. "So, can you point me in the right direction? Or take me there?"

He held her gaze for several beats, his lips quirking up at the corners. Lucy didn't want to traipse around in the almost-dark with another stranger. She had one waiting for her right in her own place, so she indicated the correct building and said, "She's in that one, around the corner, ground floor."

Seconds ticked by, and then he put out his hand. "The name's Michael. And thank you so much, Miss, Mrs....?" His voice trailed off expectantly.

Warning bells sounded even as she started to say her real name. She stumbled and improvised. "Lu—cinda P-Preston. And you're welcome." She smiled to hopefully cover her lie. But since her kidnapping she tended to be suspicious of strangers. Well, except for Jake Dalton, who she'd allowed to—

"Maybe I'll see you around, then. Thanks again, Lu—cinda." He started to turn away.

"Your welcome. Good night."

Michael headed off into the gathering evening shadows, waving a hand over his head in acknowledgement while she looked after his retreating form.

Hefting the bag of groceries, Lucy continued on her way, trudging toward the stairs as she considered the man. She supposed some women would have found him attractive, all ripped and clean-shaven as he had been, but she wasn't one of them. That didn't say much, given her track record with men, but still, he'd left her cold.

Not like Jake Dalton, with his lean yet muscular form. In those borrowed jeans that molded his legs and cupped his buttocks like they'd been made for him, he could make her mouth water on sight. Or that devilish face with just enough stubble to tickle her lips, and hair long enough to bury her hands in—

She nearly missed a step on the stairs. God, she really was hot for him. If common sense hadn't intruded at the last minute yesterday, she would have devoured him, allowed him to devour her. And beyond what he'd shown her on the internet and what she'd seen with her own eyes, she didn't know him at all.

That only made her reaction scarier. Jake was not the type of man who dated her. He was not the type of man who teased and flirted with her. He was the type of man who strolled unseeingly past her with a size zero platinum blonde clinging to his arm, her bra size larger than her IQ.

Lucy knew the status quo by now, and really wasn't bothered by it too much. She knew her place in the dating world, and it was with the Jobless Bobs, the guys who were willing to overlook her bespectacled face and overripe shape. Until now. Now, she found herself thinking, hoping, and wishing the status quo would suddenly change, specifically because of the man currently hiding out in her apartment.

And, yup, she was back to those crazy thoughts again.

Reaching the landing, Lucy noted with a growling stomach that someone was having a good dinner from the smells swirling around her. When she unlocked the front door, she realized the delicious aroma came from her place.

She stopped on the threshold. Nearly leaned out and checked the number of her apartment. But she was in the right place. And then the man that took up way too much of her thoughts in too short a time poked his head around the kitchen wall and said, "Dinner's just about ready."

Closing the door, Lucy cocked her head. "You're cooking."

Jake speared her with an amused look.

"Wow, you could be a detective," he drawled, dark brows winging upwards over sparkling brown eyes. Eyes that she remembered boring into hers last night, inviting her to let go of her inhibitions.

As she hung back by the entrance, Jake approached with deliberate steps, his gaze unswerving. Taking the grocery bag from her frozen fingers he said quietly, "Forget about last night, Lucy. I was ready. You weren't. End of story. Don't get embarrassed."

She studied his face, recognized sincerity in his expression, and felt the tightness in her stomach ease. Not ready to speak yet, she gave a quick nod and edged around him. She'd nearly reached the bedroom when he continued, "But, for future reference, make sure you tell me when you *are* ready, sweetheart. Because you wanted me, *that* much I know. You just weren't ready to act on it. And I can deal with that."

She stumbled on her way to her room, recovered, and shut the door between them with force. She leaned against it. Oh God, he knew she'd been ready to give in last night. On the heels of that thought came another. Of course he had, stupid. What girl lets a man stick his hands down her pants unless she wants him?

But she'd stopped, because, although Jake was gorgeous and not really an escaped con, he was still on the run and most likely not going to stick around for any length of time. And Lucy was tired of transient love affairs. Besides, she hadn't been this wildly attracted to a man in ages, which made her more cautious. And a man on the run from a drug lord wasn't someone she should add to her romantic resume.

Changing into another sweat suit, Lucy smoothed her ponytail and exited the bedroom. She couldn't resist inhaling the smell of home-cooked food, and made her way to the kitchen, where she could hear her handsome roommate puttering about.

"What's cooking?" she asked, joining him at the kitchen counter. "You didn't have to, you know."

"I almost wasn't able to. Your fridge was practically empty. What do you eat, anyway? The plants in the courtyard?"

She couldn't help herself. She glanced longingly at the oven. "I usually—um—bring something home. See, the bag?" She nodded at the reusable satchel he'd placed on the counter. It was his turn to roll his eyes.

"Well, it was the least I could do after you let me spend the night. If you're ready, we'll be eating in less than five minutes. I had to guess at when you'd be home. Not bad, eh? Make a good detective myself, don't I?"

Was he flirting with her? Would he? Even after last night, when she shot his more aggressive moves down? By the way he was gently smiling, she guessed he would, and was. And the thought warmed her insides.

He'd moved to the oven while she'd been contemplating his behavior and was now pulling out a quiche. A *quiche*? All other thoughts left her head. He made a quiche out of the food in *her* fridge? Who was this man, a magician? Or, better yet, Gordon Ramsey?

Jake turned around. "Sit. It's not as good if it's cold."

Numbly, she did as she was told, sitting down with the man who'd first kidnapped her, then come to her for safety, and now had cooked her dinner. That "down the rabbit hole" feeling overtook her senses once more. Lifting her fork, she watched him seat himself across the little dinette table. Their knees almost touched beneath the tabletop.

He paused, as if sensing her consternation. One brow rose as a mocking smile flitted across his supple lips. "What?

Real men don't make quiche? Some of the best chefs are men. I've had a longer relationship with food than with most women. I started my cooking career in the high school cafeteria, carried it on into college. But I gotta admit, your kitchen was a particular challenge."

With her fork suspended, she hesitated to gaze directly into his teasing expression. But as she placed it between her lips and the delicate flavors of his thrown-together dinner exploded on her tongue, she decided now was not the time to ponder their mutual attraction. Maybe after she'd eaten.

"Oh. My. God. Oh, this is soooo…mmmm." She groaned with her eyes closed. After a few more appreciative moans of ecstasy, with no sounds returning from across the table, she lazily opened her eyelids to find her companion staring at her.

She flushed to the roots of her hair, realized her orgasmic response to the meal smacked of *When Harry Met Sally*. Oh, she was mortified. Crawl under the table and hide embarrassed. She was staring into the warm, brown eyes of the most gorgeous man in her entire acquaintance and sounding like she'd had the best sex of her life.

His gaze warmed with humor and something else. An attentiveness, a sharp realization that they were that single man and woman from last night, with nothing stopping them from acting on their attraction but her weak inhibitions. When his look shifted to predatory, she plunged another forkful of the heavenly food into her mouth, speaking around it to dispel the sexually-charged atmosphere.

"This is fantastic, Mr. Dalton. I've been so hungry and I worked through lunch. I can't help myself."

Shut up, she silently screamed. She was rambling, but

was unable to quit. The man's appearance, his talents, and the way he looked at her had her fumbling. And all the while she shoveled forkfuls into her mouth like a pie-eating contestant in the home stretch.

"It's Jake. Not Mr. Dalton. I told you, it's my way of thanking you for housing and taking care of me. It's been a while since anyone has."

She paused, caught his eyes, and took a few moments to digest his words.

"Well, knowing that you weren't actually an escaped convict helped, even though you did really scare me that day." She frowned at him over her plate, and he had the grace to look ashamed.

"I have apologized. I was hoping tonight's meal went a little way toward making amends. What else can I do to show I'm sorry?"

The image of them naked together flashed so quickly through Lucy's brain she thought it might be subliminal. She was shocked. Why would making love with Jake Dalton pop into her head as a way for him to show his sincerity? It was oh-so inappropriate and not at all what she wanted. Wasn't it? But my goodness, now that she'd imagined him without clothes she couldn't get the picture out of her head.

Shoving back her chair, she took her plate to the sink then turned around and steeled herself against his earnest expression. "Clean up the kitchen? I have some emails to answer for work." She avoided looking into his eyes as she moved past him and back toward her bedroom, picking up her closed laptop from the coffee table. Just as she cleared her doorway, she thought she heard him say, "Aye, aye, captain. I'll get right to it."

Lucy almost slammed the door in response to his mocking comeback.

Lucy lay in bed that night, staring at the ceiling and contemplating the man in the other room, as well as her unsuitable thoughts regarding him. She liked his looks, his personality—of course she did. He was hot. But why did she find herself so drawn to him that she imagined them in bed together? They'd only shared one kiss. But what a kiss...

Yes, he was right. She wanted him. Wanted him like a woman wants chocolate. If she was honest with herself, she even knew why. Unlike past suitors, Jake Dalton was comfortable being who he was. He was confident. He faced problems, didn't sit back and whine. That was majorly attractive to Lucy, who usually dated men who leaned on her for support. Add to that Jake's sexy physique, sinfully handsome face, and go-to-hell attitude, and Lucy was afraid she could fall for him in a big way, even though he was *sooo* not her type.

It was probably also the fact that he made it clear he found her attractive. Drop-dead gorgeous hunk Jake Dalton had wanted C-cup, size ten Lucy Parker enough that he would have taken her to bed last night. She'd known it and had run from it. From him, because she didn't want to be compared to all the Barbie dolls she was sure he normally surrounded himself with.

Rolling to her side and seeing the clock display a blurry eleven p.m., she sighed and scrunched her eyes shut, willing herself to sleep while trying not to think about the two of them together. But her attempts were futile, merely making her hot and bothered and confused, which didn't help her sleeplessness. So she resolutely shoved Jake Dalton with the magic lips and fingers out of her mind, and attempted to clear her brain of everything but hypnotizing thoughts of "you're getting sleepier."

Apparently the exercise worked, because she was jolted awake by an almost imperceptible noise. Checking the time, Lucy saw she'd been asleep for three hours, and wondered what she'd heard. After several moments of strained listening, she sat up.

A rapid burst of movement in the room was her only warning. Before she could respond, a sudden weight crashed down on her body. It crushed the air from her lungs and pinioned her legs under the blankets. A gloved hand slammed over her mouth, sealing it shut.

She flailed wildly under the intruder. Adrenaline rushed. This wasn't Jake. She knew it intuitively. *He'd* manhandled her enough in the past for her to know the difference. And that scared her even more, realizing she was once again being accosted by a male.

Refusing to give up, she began to bow and buck her body, anything to unseat this ski-masked home invader. She would not be a victim. She bit the hand over her mouth and won a cuffing blow to the side of her head for her efforts. She reeled, saw stars behind her eyelids, but still she continued her thrashing.

And all the while the gloved hand held her breath captive, the heavy body pressing her down, squeezing the air from her lungs. She felt faint from lack of oxygen and the glancing pain at her temple. Her movements slowed. Vision swam. She was suffocating. She was going to die. Right here, right now, with Jake only steps away in the other room. How ironic.

Unexpectedly, her attacker shifted, and there was air. Fresh, heaven-sent air, gulped in through a suddenly exposed nose, though her mouth remained covered. Rejuvenated, she redoubled her bucking efforts, grunted through the human gag as she tried to unseat her attacker.

Only to freeze when she spied the knife brandished before her eyes, its blade gleaming in the bluish glow of her bedside alarm clock.

She stiffened. Eyes locking on the weapon, sweat broke out all over her body. Tremors of fear shook her. This was it. All the fighting for her rights, all the picking herself up by the bootstraps, this was where it would end. She whimpered, teeth chattering.

Her assailant chuckled sadistically as he drew the knife's point down her temple in a deadly, arrow-straight line. His eyes tracked the path of the blade and the thin line of blood it left behind.

He licked his lips and leaned in close. "Do you think he'll make a trade, you fat cow? Do you matter at all to Nicky, I wonder? Stop fighting and come with me now, or I'll carve your eyes out."

Chapter Nine

Jake awakened a little before two. He lay listening to the silence inside and outside the apartment. On a sigh, he sat up and grabbed the TV remote. Time to channel surf. Maybe he'd find something to take his mind off the sexy accountant he spent way too much time fantasizing about.

He'd found out she was an accountant earlier today, when she'd gone to work and he'd been trapped inside the apartment. First, he'd showered again, because he couldn't get enough of all that hot water. Then he'd eaten and turned on the TV for news of the ongoing manhunt for Nicky Costas. He was relieved to see it had been buried fifteen minutes into the news hour. The pursuit was still going on, but in the mountains. His captain had kept his word and limited the press exposure.

He'd moved on to the laptop, searching for something, anything he could find to support his hunch that he was being set up. He hit brick wall after brick wall, though, without the use of his official credentials, so he'd shoved the laptop aside and started snooping on his hot hostess.

He learned that she was an extremely neat person, which was a bitch because it meant he had to put back her mail and other paperwork exactly as he found it. He'd discovered she worked for a tax accounting firm in the city and drew a decent salary. She had a nice little nest egg in a savings account, and he wondered what she was saving for. A trip? A house? He shouldn't be so interested.

She didn't have an overabundance of personal relationships, that was for sure. The one he did find was with a Mary Alton who couldn't seem to pay her rent on time or in full. Lucy had pitched in a couple hundred dollars on more than one occasion.

He came to the conclusion that Lucy never let her hair down and he found himself speculating what had made her so…businesslike. With her looks and body, she should be rotating hot dates in and out of her place on a conveyor belt. But, except for him, there was no evidence of a steady man, or any man, in her life. By her own admission she'd had an "ex," but from the pics on her Facebook page there didn't seem to have been anyone since. And he wanted to know why.

As Jake now punched in his favorite TV channels and received black screens with the encouragement to "subscribe today" he realized Lucy also didn't splurge on any of the good channels. Some more of that thriftiness he'd discovered over the course of his day. That figured. She had the body of a goddess and the scruples of a nun.

Not willing to stoop to watching infomercials, Jake tossed the remote aside, stood up, and stretched. Lucy Parker was turning into a problem. As much as he was grateful for a place to stay, she was influencing his thoughts and actions way too much, and that was dangerous for him. Dangerous because he needed to concentrate on this muddle of a case, and instead he found himself trying to impress her as a police officer, as a cook, and, most of all, as a man.

Crossing the floor to check the door lock he asked himself since when had he cared if there were napkins on the table under the proper utensil? Or that the dishes matched? When did he ever walk back into a bathroom to make sure he'd put the toilet seat down and hadn't left a mini Lake Erie dripping off the sink counter?

It felt odd considering another person in this way. Odd, but also right, like he'd grown beyond hiding behind a dysfunctional family and was finally able to share himself with another human being. Which was really screwed-up thinking when he was wanted by both a drug lord and the department he worked for. What woman would want to tie herself to him?

Deciding the subject was just too deep to contemplate at this time of night, and that pacing the apartment wasn't solving anything, Jake decided to get a bowl of cereal. Maybe a full stomach would help him fall asleep.

He'd reached the kitchen when he paused and tilted his head, convinced he'd heard a strange sound from Lucy's bedroom. Or was it wishful thinking? The gentleman buried deep inside him insisted he move on, but his cop's sixth sense had him easing the bedroom door open anyway.

The first thing he spied were two bodies in the center of the bed. Adrenaline surged and he saw red. On a growl, he launched himself at the shadowed figure straddling Lucy, snagging the assailant's throat in one tight-fingered grasp and hauling him up and off of her.

The intruder swung around, right arm outstretched. He had a knife. Lightning quick, Jake grabbed his attacker's wrist with one hand and twisted until the guy's arm bent backward. Jake pinched down on the dude's pressure point until he heard the clunk of the blade on the floor over their raspy breathing. Trying to see in the dark where it fell so he wouldn't slice up his bare feet, he was caught off guard with a punch to his cheekbone that snapped his head back. That pissed him off.

Like a crazed bull, Jake head-butted his adversary. The guy barely grunted when Jake connected with his iron-hard abs, though the assault sent them crashing into Lucy's dresser. Items shattered.

Recovering first, Jake grabbed the intruder by his shoulders and kneed him in the groin. A hiss of indrawn breath told him he'd scored. Buoyed, Jake clenched his fist and drew back, throwing a heavy punch to the guy's face. His connection was solid, twanging right up his arm.

In retaliation, Lucy's attacker reached up and boxed Jake's ears. Jake jack-knifed forward, his hearing fading and eyesight blurring. Doubled over, he managed to brace for the uppercut he saw coming. The one-two blow had him seeing stars. This guy was no amateur.

Swaying upright, Jake shook off his residual dizziness and deflected the dude's next shot with a forearm block, parrying with a quick jab to his neck. A strangled cough meant he'd done some damage. One quick glance to the side told him that Lucy had left the bed, but he had no idea where she was in the dark room. Likewise, he couldn't distinguish much about the intruder, except that he was near Jake's own height, but way more bulked up. And he fought like a pro.

The guy swung his left leg toward Jake's face, and Jake automatically caught it. And yanked. Hard. The man should have toppled. Instead, he jumped into the air and clocked Jake in the head with his free foot, dropping him to the floor.

Shaking off wooziness, Jake pulled himself to all fours. Out of the corner of his eye he saw his opponent draw back his foot. Jake punched the guy in the side of the kneecap. The dude fell like Goliath.

Jake jumped on him, throwing punches to the intruder's masked face like his arms were pistons. The man rolled side to side, trying to unseat him. Jake retaliated, grabbing his opponent's collar and slamming his head into the floor. The shithead swore, then raised his pelvis high enough that Jake slipped to the side. He tried to wrestle Jake under him, but Jake jerked free, jabbing at the guy's eyes with his fingers. The man attempted to knee him in the groin.

"Get out of the way, Jake, I've got your gun!" Lucy shouted from across the room.

The guy's head popped up at the sound of her voice, and so did Jake's. Holy shit, she really was holding the Beretta. She was pointing it at the two of them with both hands clasped around the butt. The gun bounced so much in her shaky grasp that if she did fire, *he'd* likely be the one to catch the bullet.

In that split second of inattention, the intruder shoved Jake off him and bolted for the window. Jake made a wild lunge for the guy's legs, but the asshole expected it. He jumped into the air, bringing his knees to his chest and out of Jake's reach. The leap landed him closer to the window, which he swung out of, grabbing onto tree branches and shimmying out of sight.

Silence. That, and the chorus of their heavy breathing filled the room. Lucy's attacker had come as he'd gone. Swift and lethal like a tornado, leaving almost as much destruction in his wake.

Jake sat back on his heels, staring out the gaping window. He'd taken precautions in this place, had kept the windows locked shut, the blinds pulled. He'd told Lucy to do the same. The guy had wanted in bad. He'd come prepared with the right tools to gain entrance.

So Jake contemplated their next move. Because they had to move. Now that someone had found him here, with Lucy, neither of them was safe. So he had to come up with a new plan. One he'd formulated last night. But, in light of what just happened, he wouldn't be doing it alone.

Rolling to his feet he turned his attention to Lucy with the now dangling gun.

"I'm gonna call the cops."

His head snapped up at the stupidest comment he'd ever heard. Unfortunately, it was coming out of the mouth of the girl he had the hots for.

Turning his head to look at her, he summoned his reserve patience. "You can't call the cops, unless you plan on telling them everything. Besides, you little fool, I *am* the cops."

"Stop calling me names. I'm sick of being called names." To his horror, Lucy broke down and began crying that foghorn cry he'd been subjected to when he'd first kidnapped her. She huddled up into the corner between the bathroom and bedroom doors, slid down the wall, and dropped her face to her drawn-up knees, wailing.

Robot-like, Jake rose to his feet and stared at her in the corner. He felt his heart drop. Instead of her blubbering annoying him like before, now her tears wounded him to his very core. His words were the cause of her grief and he didn't like that realization. All he could think of was alleviating her anguish and fear.

He walked over to Lucy and hunkered down before her. After a brief hesitation, he sat beside her and pulled her into his lap. She resisted momentarily, but then leaned into him. Still sobbing, she buried her face against his chest and wept. His arms found their way around her.

"He—he cut me. He—he said he would c-cut my eyes out."

An icy cold sluiced over Jake. Gently he pushed her back from him so he could look into her face. It was hard to do, since she hiccupped every once in a while and tears still tracked down her face. But there it was: a thin, thin line of blood, pink now that it had mixed with her tears, slicing down the side of her face like a scalpel cut.

Rage, deep and sick and thick, boiled up from the depths of his angry soul as he studied the mark. Someone would pay for this, he vowed. Someone would pay dearly.

However, a lot of that blame belonged squarely on his shoulders, since he was the one who first involved her in this game of deceit. The admission was hard to accept. He took a thumb and gently wiped at the streaks of blood.

"I'm sorry, Lucy, for involving you. For scaring you. For getting you cut. It won't leave a scar. Not on your face, at least. But I'm afraid it's left one on me."

As her wet, brown gaze met his, he felt his insides start to crumble. Jesus, those out-of-focus doe eyes slayed him with their misery. He felt like the most worthless piece of shit on the planet for causing her this distress. To comfort her, and to hide his guilt from her wide-eyed innocence, he pressed her head back to his shoulder and began rocking her in his arms. "I'm sorry I snapped at you."

"H-he called me a fat cow. That h-hurt more than the kn-knife." This came muffled against his shirt, but Jake heard the comment plainly and once more a dark, filthy anger rose up, nearly choking him in its intensity. Fat? A cow? Was the asshole blind?

By Jake's expert assessment, Lucy possessed the old Hollywood style of body, before they all became emaciated. No, Lucy wasn't fat, or bovine. She was soft where she needed to be soft, and, damn, right now he was hard when he didn't need to be hard.

Pressing a chaste kiss on the top of her head, he attempted humor. "The only one remotely like a cow, Lucy, is that douchebag, because when I hunt him down, I'm gonna butcher him like prime beef." He felt her smile against his chest, and it was like she'd exonerated him. Since when had his moods become dependent on hers?

The thought niggled at him, a warning he couldn't take the time to dissect. Instead, he looked at her downturned head. "You know, we have to leave. He will come back and he'll bring reinforcements. We don't have much time."

She stiffened in his arms.

He'd broken the spell.

Lucy slid off Jake's lap as she digested his words. Leave? Leave her home, her belongings, and just run away? Could she do that? Didn't she have to? Did she want to stay behind and risk another attack?

She shuddered at the memory of that man lying on her, knife to her face, and she realized she would do what Jake told her because it was her only choice.

"What do I have to do?" she asked slowly, wrapping her arms around herself after realizing she was sitting near him in nothing but boy shorts and her thin tank top without a bra. His eyes dropped to her chest and then bounced back to her face.

"Get a duffel bag or backpack, pack it with important papers you don't want to lose, get some clothes and underwear and shit, and be ready to rock and roll in five. Someone could have heard all this. Okay?"

She stared at him a moment before turning to the closet and grabbing some clothes and the other items he'd mentioned. When he left the room to give her privacy, she paused. This was really happening. She was running for her life, leaving behind everything familiar to her, running alongside the very man who'd brought this all crashing down on the two of them. The thought was not encouraging.

"We'll hit the bank a couple times, but it'll have to be at various branches," he said, reentering the bedroom as she came out of the closet. She'd put on a gray sweatshirt and black jeans, and pulled her hair back into a ponytail.

"H—how long will we be gone?"

He held her gaze, visibly tamping down his impatience to blow this place. After all, he'd been living this life since he'd escaped from prison. "Sweetheart, kiss this place good-bye."

Her chin trembled as she glanced around the space she'd occupied the last few years. The place she'd called home. Their eyes met again.

"Will—will it get blown up?"

He gave a short shake of his head. "Probably not. But it'll get tossed pretty seriously. Don't know if you'd want to move back in afterwards. That asshole wanted to use you to get to me. Must have had a tail on me, which brings up some interesting questions." He went silent, his gaze distant.

Lucy didn't care about the questions or the tail he mentioned. She wanted nothing more than to wake up and realize this was all a bad dream. But she knew it wasn't a dream. It was a living nightmare, and the only solution was standing in front of her in jeans and a cotton t-shirt, with two-toned hair and a scruffy chin.

"L—let me get a jacket and I'll be ready." She ducked into the closet and returned with her black coat. Meeting his eyes once more, she stopped when he put a hand on her upper arm.

"Lucy." He sucked in a deep breath. "I'm sorry like hell for dragging you into this. I mean it. I wasn't thinking beyond myself when I ran off that work crew that day. All I knew was I had to get out of there. I never thought how it might affect other people. I'm sorry. I'm sorry for kidnapping you, terrorizing you, and most of all, for tonight." He reached out and once more touched her face, where the slightly puffy line still ached.

In that moment, Lucy knew that she could fall for this man in a big way. Maybe she already had. She could ignore the facts, even fight the attraction. Or she could accept the

Lucy Parker curse of always finding an ineligible male and follow this attraction as far as it went. Probably to a lifetime behind bars, at least for him. Mentally shaking her head at the irony of it all, she inhaled sharply and took the plunge into the symbolic deep end that yawned before her.

"What's done is done, isn't it? We'd better go while we can." She moved around him and headed for the apartment's front door, never looking back.

Jake parked Lucy's car at the bus station before dawn, and they stripped it clean. Not that it needed much. Accountants were tidy people by nature, he'd discovered. As they locked the little car, their eyes met and she asked, "What next?"

He'd been lost in thought as they had driven first to the post office, where he went in and this time successfully opened the PO box Jerry had insisted on getting despite Jake's protests. The scrap of paper inside had an address and code written on it. Also in the box was a single key on a ring. The items only gave him more questions.

Then they'd gone to an ATM and withdrawn the maximum amount Lucy could for the day. Coupled with his meager stash in his backpack, they had enough to live on, if that living was frugal, because he was pretty damn sure his as well as "Nicky's" bank accounts were being watched, if they weren't already frozen.

Once more he gazed over at Lucy. She looked cute in her sweatshirt, jeans, and pink baseball cap with her ponytail drawn through the hole in the back. She really turned him on, from that innocent vulnerability that had him wanting to slay dragons for her, right to those glasses that slid down her nose when she cried. He'd never dated a woman who wore glasses. He wondered if the lenses steamed up when she kissed, if she kept them on while she had sex…

Shit. They'd both been beaten up this morning, and now he was thinking of steamy sex? His priorities were definitely skewed. Making out was probably the last thing on her mind right now. He wrinkled his nose and came around the car, careful to keep his wayward hands away from her, lest they start roving all over those bumps and curves she camouflaged under baggy clothes.

He led her away from the deserted bus station. And heard her scramble to catch up. When she came abreast of him, he replied to her earlier question.

"Next? Next, we walk."

"No buses?"

"Nope."

She had to trot to keep up with his determined strides.

"Well, where are we walking *to*?"

Jake looked down into her face and grinned slowly before pointing at the U Store It sign a block away on the same side of the street. "We're going right there, sweetheart."

He turned to continue, but she ground to a halt, pulling on his hand. "Why?"

Oh, hell. Wasn't that usually the way with intelligent women? They always had to slow the process down with questions instead of just trusting the man. But the thought that he might owe her some explanations had him pushing her back into the shade of a brick building.

"A few months ago," he said, "Jerry told me he'd gotten

a PO box under a fake name. I think I mentioned that to you already. Anyway, I advised him it wasn't a good idea. No paper trails, but he told me to stop being his dad. That he knew what he was doing.

"He insisted on giving me the number of the box, since I wouldn't take the key. Told me there might come a time that he wouldn't be around to have my back. That's when I would need what that box holds. I told him to stop talking crap. When I escaped I remembered that conversation and found the box, but I couldn't get into it at the time. That's why we just went to the post office. I managed to pick its lock."

He didn't add that he'd studied how to do it on YouTube while sitting on her sofa. That skill wasn't exactly one taught at the academy. "This is what was inside." He held up the key ring with the U Store It logo as well as the piece of paper.

"Since this is the only U Store It facility in town, chances are we're in the right place. If ever there was a time we might need some extra help, now would be it." He hoped to God that his cop instincts were correct: that Jerry had left a clue, perhaps evidence that he'd stumbled upon outside of their investigation that might give Jake an edge.

Looking up, he found Lucy staring into his face. He'd piqued her curiosity, apparently.

"Do you think it might be money?" she asked.

"Could be." He guided her across the street up to the storage yard perimeter gate. He punched in the code that was written on the paper and, after an ominous clink, the wrought iron gate started sliding open. One step closer to some of the answers to his questions. His pulse sped up at the thought that within minutes he might know why he'd been set up. Maybe even by whom.

Advancing into the storage unit area and glancing at the number on one side of the key, he adjusted their direction to follow the numbers on the corresponding units.

"Why rent such a big space?" she asked. "He could have used a safe deposit box for money."

"Good question." Their feet crunched on the blacktop, the only sound in this maze of identical, orange garage doors. She sidled closer to him, and he angled himself behind her slightly in case of a rear attack.

"Ah-ha, here it is." He stopped in front of unit 165 and paused, reached under his shirt at his back, and withdrew his Beretta. Lucy's eyes grew wide.

"Wh—why do you need that?" She looked around the empty area, then back at him.

"Hopefully I don't. Need it, that is. But with Jerry's apartment and the attack at your place, that means we have a tail. If there's a welcome party for us, I'd feel a helluva lot better if you waited over there in the shadows than right beside me."

"You really think—"

"Just get out of the way, Lucy, and run like hell if something happens. And here, take this." He shrugged off the backpack and handed it to her. She took it like an automaton, still in shock at his words. But, shit, he really didn't know what to expect in the next few minutes. He hoped he was just being overly cautious.

After all, they'd hit the ground running after Lucy's attack, and he'd made sure to cover their trail by looping through the city before coming here. But he couldn't rule out that someone had followed them and was just waiting for him to open the door. His only hope (*their* only hope) was that Farelli thought he knew the whereabouts of his stolen money, so that killing him was not an option. Yet. His heartbeat tripled.

Seeing that Lucy had done as he'd told her, he directed his attention to the lock. Put the key inside and turned it. Then he took a deep breath, tightened his hold on the Beretta, and rolled the door up, jumping to the side once it cleared the level of his head.

Lucy gasped.

Chapter Ten

Before him, illuminated by the lighted driveway markers, sat the newest, shiniest, blackest Porsche 911 Turbo S he'd ever laid eyes on. A serious driving machine.

It begged him to take it for a spin.

Entering the unit, gun still at the ready, he circled the Porsche, trailing a hand along its sleek lines, shaking his head at Jerry's choice of car, his extravagance. It was a testimony to how his friend had lived his life, and a testimony to their past friendship, that this vehicle sat here now, waiting for Jake.

He stepped back and simply stared, mind tunneling back through his and Jerry's relationship, all the way to the early years, before duty and greed and dishonor destroyed their friendship.

"A car? Are you serious? He left you a car?"

Jake snapped back into the present. He swung around while shoving his gun into the back of his pants, thoughts of what he and Jerry could have accomplished together disintegrating.

Seeing that he was still in one piece, she had followed him into the unit and was now standing before the car with an unimpressed look on her face.

"It's not *just a car,* my dear woman," he tried to explain. "This is a Porsche. A highly tuned, extremely sensitive piece of equipment made for only the most serious of drivers. Calling it a car is like calling the...the Hope Diamond just a diamond."

She wasn't buying it. He could tell by the way she frowned, by the way she cocked her head. She didn't agree with Jerry's choice of repayment for his past transgressions and mistakes. But hell, what did she know? Cars were for men what shoes were for women.

"At least the Hope Diamond doesn't lose its value. Didn't this—this Jerry know that a car depreciates in value as soon as you drive it off the lot? That no matter whether it's a Honda or a Porsche, it will lose fifteen to twenty percent of its value in just the first year, and in subsequent ye—"

"Enough. Let me bask in the moment here without your financial mumbo jumbo that's sure to bring a dark cloud along any minute. Besides, it's a *Porsch-a*, not a *Porshe*."

"Whatever," she mumbled, shuffling back and tilting her head at him. That's when he noticed the shadows beneath her eyes, the tightness of her mouth. She looked ready to drop from stress and lack of sleep, and here he was, her would-be hero, practically making out with this car.

Yeah. Time to go.

He knelt by a tire. Felt up into its wheel well and then moved to the next wheel to do the same when he didn't find what he wanted. Before she could ask what he was looking for he stood and grinned in satisfaction, brandishing a key. He clicked the fob, and the car chirped twice, flashing brilliant headlights.

Whatever else Jerry had become, he'd had good taste in automobiles. As Jake opened the driver's door, the new car smell assaulted them, and they both involuntarily breathed deep. Lucy crept up to his side.

"Couldn't resist, could you?" he asked mischievously.

She rolled her eyes. "I never said I didn't like the car, or its smell. It's just, if Jerry was going to help you in the future, why didn't he buy a restaurant, or a building with this money? Why a fancy, sporty car that can be traced?"

Good question, Jake said in his head. But then, Jerry probably hadn't figured on dying. He'd probably wanted to keep the car for himself, since Jake wasn't supposed to know about it unless something happened to Jerry. Jake shook his head. There was only one thing he was completely sure of, and that was that his long-time friend and partner had gathered the money for the car by stealing from Farelli. A good cop would never have had the money for a Porsche.

But to Lucy he said, "Jerry always was a sucker for Porsches."

"Well, besides driving it and drawing attention to you in the process, I don't see a lot of good it will do."

Frustrated and tired, he said, "Hell, I don't know what he was thinking, Lucy. I'm just as puzzled as you."

"I'm not trying to make you angry."

Aww, shit. Here she was, on the run with all her worldly possessions stuffed in a backpack, a cut on her face from a knife wielded by someone out to catch *him,* and she was apologizing to him? He was the cause of all the upheaval in her life and *she* was sorry? He was an asshole, plain and simple.

He reached out and pulled her to him in a one-armed hug, dropped a kiss on top of that cute, pink hat before releasing her. "I'm not angry, Luce. Never at you. I'm angry at the situation, and at myself for getting you involved. You're right. I wasn't expecting a car any more than you were. But maybe there's a clue."

He immediately bent down into the open driver's door and spied an envelope on the black leather passenger seat. *Oh, hell*, he thought, knowing it would be a message from his former friend. He wasn't sure how he would react to seeing Jerry's handwriting from the grave.

He barely noticed Lucy move away to slump cross-legged on the concrete floor as he sat in the driver's seat and carefully slit open the envelope. He found a stack of slightly used, one hundred-dollar bills nestled inside.

Jake stared, then numbly folded the wad and slipped it into his hoodie pocket. Then he turned his reluctant attention to the letter written in Jerry's slashed style of writing, immersing himself in what might well be his friend's last living words.

Jake,

Well, shit, bro, if you're reading this it means I'm gone. Toast. Off into the great unknown. And that sucks for me. But anyway, gotta keep this short and to the point. No cry baby stuff, you hear? You've been like a brother to me, man, and I want you to know that.

This car is yours. I know you wanted that restaurant, but hey, a Porsche is amazing, and I was hoping to be around to drive it. But I'm not, I guess, so it's yours. After all, you couldn't run the restaurant without me, so that makes this the better investment. At least I think so.

It's clean. Completely paid for. No hassles for you. I made sure of that. And it isn't hot, either, so you don't have to drive it looking over your shoulder all the time. Enjoy it, and think of me while you're driving it. The money here is a down payment for all the shit I've put you through. Check the glovebox in case that shit gets violent.

I'm sorry I was never as strong as you, Jake. But you knew that all our lives, didn't you? You've protected me from myself forever, bro, but I guess everything finally caught up with me. It's been great being your friend and partner. Now go on out there and fight the good fight. I'll be fine.

Jerry

The words on the paper blurred as Jake's eyes filled, the tears trickling down his cheeks because of his dead friend's joking farewell. He swiped his face angrily while blinking furiously.

"Damn it, Jer. Why'd you go and get yourself killed, you dumb-ass? You point a gun at me and then you hand me a frickin' racecar. Now I'm left holding the bag." Obviously, Jerry had written this before Jake last saw him. *The least you coulda done was tell me who was skimming off the top.* Shit. He pinched the bridge of his nose, hard, and attempted to stave off the rush of more tears. It truly was his last, best moment with his late childhood friend.

A gentle hand touched his shoulder. "Jake? Are you all right?"

He blinked rapidly, holding up the letter without making a sound. He couldn't choke any words past the lump of sorrow anyway. She took in the letter and her gaze softened.

"It's okay to cry for your friend, Jake. You two had a long history, right?"

Gazing out the windshield, he nodded.

Studying Jake's shaggy head, Lucy felt an odd stirring within, similar to attraction, but something more. She knew she was drawn to him, had come to terms with the realization after that steamy kiss they'd shared. But now she also felt a—a *protective* feeling toward him. She wanted to hold him like he'd held her after she'd been attacked. Comfort him and tell him everything would be all right even though she had no idea whether it ever would be again.

And then he raised his head, eyes glistening, a lopsided smirk crossing his face.

"If you tell anyone—*anyone*—about this, I'll categorically deny it, and even lock your sexy ass in jail for slander, Lucy."

She raised her brows above her glasses frames, surprised at his mercurial mood change. And cracked a relieved smile in return.

Just like that, they were back on even ground.

Leaning forward, he opened the glovebox. And whistled. He pulled out a gun. A blunt-nosed, fit-in-the-palm-of-your-hand gun. Great, another weapon. Lucy slid back, not comfortable around it. Closing the box, Jake pushed out of the driver's seat, wiped his eyes once, and pocketed the firearm. Then he folded the letter and put it with the gun.

"Jerry just leveled the playing field for us." She caught

his look and watched as he once more circled the Porsche. A thoughtful expression passed over his face; it warned her he was thinking again, and thinking hard. So she stood silently, watching him as he paced.

At last he stopped and studied the car. "This falls right into the plan I was hatching. It's as if Jerry was still working this case."

"What plan? You have a plan?" She sounded skeptical even to herself, but he just laughed.

"Yeah, I do. It's a road trip, sweetheart, so jump in for the ride of your life." He moved around to the driver's side of the Porsche.

"Where to?" she asked suspiciously, never one to blindly obey. He should know that by now about her. His grin widened.

"Vegas, baby. We're going to Vegas."

Lucy slept through a good portion of the desert drive, the events from the night before catching up to her. Jake didn't help matters by rambling on about The Car, as she dubbed it in her mind. It shifted so smoothly, it was so aerodynamic, it had enough horsepower it could—yada, yada, yada. Soon she drifted off, leaving him to admire the vehicle in silence.

Four hours later, she stood in the lobby of the Continental Hotel on the Las Vegas Strip, a grandiose resort and casino of Italian-inspired design, complete with a canal and real gondolas cruising outside and inside the hotel. Hordes of tourists crammed the huge carpeted and marble lobby. A cacophony of languages and conversations surrounded her.

She contemplated why they were here while she waited in the check-in line. Jake hadn't told her much, and then she'd fallen asleep. It didn't sound like a good idea to use the money from his dead partner, so she pulled out the cash she'd retrieved after the attack in her apartment. Spending stolen money might send Jake to jail for real this time.

There was that protective feeling again, the one that had started back in the storage unit. It had been her downfall in the past, but this time she swore it felt different. Jake Dalton was the type of man who could accept an independent woman. He'd come to her when he was out of options, hadn't he? Of course, he was also the one who had initially involved her in this mess, but she couldn't imagine herself sitting this out. Whatever happened next, she wanted to be around, even if it meant she would be in danger. And that told her...

Her head started to throb and Lucy rubbed her forehead. She knew Jake wanted to "follow the money," as he'd put it when they'd started out from the storage facility, but right now she just wanted to lie down. Close her eyes and escape reality for a while.

She stammered her way through the check-in process when she got to the counter. She used her ID since Jake had none. He was leaning against the far wall, head down, trying to look inconspicuous. Any minute now she was sure hotel security would barge in and grab him. Wasn't there a manhunt still going on for Nicky Costas? Her palms began to sweat at the thought, her knees started to tremble.

"You're all set, Ms. Parker. Enjoy your stay."

Lucy blinked at the clerk then nodded quickly, grabbing the key and hustling away. She slowed as she approached

Jake, taking a moment to study him before he was aware of her presence. Her fear receded slightly when she realized he looked like every other guy here in the lobby. Blue jeans, sneakers, sunglasses, and a backpack. No one could see the guns he'd hidden inside the pack. Or the money he'd inherited from a friend who'd been killed by a sniper's bullet—

"Take a picture, it'll last longer."

She hadn't realized she was staring until he spoke, saying the words he'd said to her the day he'd jumped into her car. She felt her face heat. He smiled at her, though she couldn't see his eyes through the dark glasses. That one crooked smile from him eased her tension. No one was coming to arrest him right now. They were just a couple checking in for a few days of gambling and shows.

"C'mon, the elevators are this way," he said, taking the key card she offered. She fell into step beside him.

The clamor of video slots followed them all the way to the bank of elevators, past a guard checking for room cards, right into the carpeted elevator occupied by about five other tourists.

She closed her eyes, listening to the music piped in around them, its soothing sound lulling her. The short nap she'd had in the car had done little to counter her overwhelming fatigue. After the elevator chimed their floor, she lagged behind Jake toward their room.

"Here we are, sweetheart. Home sweet home." He swung open the door, allowing her to enter before him. She ground to a halt just over the threshold, causing him to run into her.

"What's wrong?" He pushed her toward the wall, his body moving ahead, physically shielding her. "Lucy?"

No, there was no imminent danger. Well, notwithstanding the man beside her.

He moved briskly through the suite, checking for threats. She stood numbly by the door.

"Come on, sweetheart." He took her hand, guiding her into the suite where one plush, king-sized bed commanded attention. Beautifully coiffed in golds, silvers, and creams, the bed boasted curtains that matched the window coverings, as well as the gold velvet couches and settee.

"There's only one bed," she pointed out unnecessarily.

He pushed past her, stepping down from the bed section into the sitting area and flopping the backpack onto one of the golden couches. He grabbed a remote off the wall and pointed it at the window draperies while explaining, "There's one in the couch, too." He pressed the remote, and the curtains at the window drew back automatically. She stared at the extravagance, rooted where she stood.

"How do you know? Have you been here before?"

He turned from the partial view of the Strip and studied her. She shut up, immediately self-conscious and exhausted. Pacing back toward her, he stayed on the lower level. "Yes, when I come to Vegas, I stay here. All the rooms are suites. That's why I like this hotel. And since we needed to come here, why not be comfortable?

"Now that we're here, why don't you take a nap, while I go to that gas station my boss said the marked money showed up at. You look wiped out, and that's my fault. You should be safe, and I won't be long—"

"You want me to take a nap?" Her eyes goggled, voice rising. "You jump in my car, parade me around the mountains, lead a hitman to my door, the mob boss you worked for is searching for you, and now you want me to take a nap while you go play detective? What happens if they find you out there? How am I going to know if you're okay? If you think I'm the only one who needs a nap, think again. But the problem is, you're *not* thinking."

Lucy stared at him from the step above, although he was so much taller, their positions put them at eye level. All the worry, the fear, and exhaustion exploded within her. She had to make him understand that this harebrained idea didn't just affect him. It also involved her. In a big way. He couldn't just bound into her life, make her start to fall for him, and then make a decision that could take him away from her forever. No, he couldn't. And she was going to tell him so.

She about-faced and strode toward the room's door before pivoting to look back at him. And then she felt the embarrassing burn of tears. Not now. Not *now*.

"You've dragged me into this mess, Jake, forced me to leave my home, my car, my job, my *life,* and now you're going to strand me in another state, with a 'hot' car and even hotter money, just so you can play James Bond? I don't think so."

O—kuuy, Jake thought to himself, shifting his feet in the uncomfortable silence. So, she was pissed. Seriously pissed. Like in, take-a-knife-and-carve-him-a-tattoo pissed.

But, this is what he did for a living. Follow leads, clear up inconsistencies. Keep the innocent safe. That's why he'd brought her along, wasn't it? Oh, hell, who was he kidding? Yes, he'd brought Lucy along to safeguard her, but he also hadn't wanted to say good-bye yet. Not after that kiss they'd shared. Not after they'd spent a day getting to know each other, living as a couple, even if it had been pretend.

Shit, being honest with himself was giving him a headache. Or maybe it was the twenty-four hours of being awake. He rubbed his forehead and wondered if the sexy accountant was right. Maybe they both needed some downtime before moving on with the investigation. But he was so close, knew he was on the right track. All he needed…

Jake cocked his head, unable to finish the thought as he stared at Lucy's bowed head. Was she…crying?

Feeling his heart crumble, he moved closer to Lucy, who definitely was emitting mewling sounds. Nothing like her foghorn wails. But still, it bothered him to see her upset.

Damn it all to hell. What was he supposed to do now? He had no experience with crying females. They were supposed to cry *after* he left, leave him oblivious to their grief—not that he'd invested enough time with any female to give her a reason to waste tears on him. He wasn't supposed to be put through this turmoil.

But this was Lucy, not some "what happens in Vegas" bimbo he'd picked up by the Wheel of Fortune slots and chosen as his "nail-ee" for the night. Lucy, of the poor self-image and the razor-sharp brain. The girl who thought on her feet and didn't take his bullshit. The accountant with the body that could steal his attention away from the Porsche downstairs just by standing next to it. This was the person he'd reduced to tears.

He lowered his hand to her shoulder. "Lucy?" He tried to peer into her face, but her cupped hands hid her from view.

He blundered on, navigating uncharted waters with someone whom he feared he was becoming seriously attached to, if how he felt right now was any indication. "I'm—I'm sorry for bringing you into this mess. I really am. I've told you that, and I'm telling you again. I wish I'd never jumped into your car—"

Quick as that, she spun around, shoved him backward with two fists to his chest. "I wish you hadn't. Then I wouldn't have to worry about you going off by yourself to solve this case. I wouldn't have to wonder if you'll be shot or killed. I wouldn't have to *care* about you."

She gave one last mighty push, sending him stumbling back. He kept his hands at his sides, accepting her tirade as his due. When she stopped pushing him away, he swallowed hard, anticipating the reaming out that he so sorely deserved. "Damn it, Jake. I wish I hadn't fallen for you."

He didn't know what shocked him more: the fact that conservative Lucy Parker had used a swear word, or the fact that, contrary to all that had come before, she grabbed the front of his shirt and hauled him to her, latching her lips on to his in a desperation-fueled kiss that rocked his world.

He had been kissed by dozens of women over the years. A good portion of them had initiated the act, too. And maybe they'd been more skilled with their mouths than an accountant with a penchant for choosing losers, but never had Jake lost control so completely, so quickly, as when Lucy Parker at last surrendered to their mutual attraction.

The moment she grabbed hold of his shoulders he free fell into the kiss, a smokejumper leaping without a chute, knowing full well he'd be consumed by the inferno but craving the heat.

With only a few nips and scrapes of her teeth, her mouth shot him right to that flashpoint of white-hot desire. God, he wanted to take command of this embrace, but it was so damned sexy, so frickin' *hot* to be on the receiving end of a woman losing control.

When he lifted his head to inhale some much needed air, her fingertips let go of his shirt and dove to the back of his head, angling his mouth for better access. Once more their lips fused together.

Wanting to anchor himself before he exploded right where he stood, Jake placed his hands at her back, impatient fingertips roving over her sweatshirt. And still she held him to her, plunging her tongue into his mouth, shocking a groan of pure, dark lust from deep within him.

His inner fight for restraint shattered. He ran his hands up beneath that bulky sweatshirt, growled appreciatively into her mouth at the feel of her hot skin under his fingertips.

In a second, she drew back, chest heaving, tears drying on her cheeks. Her glasses were steamed. *There was the answer to that question*, he noted as he gulped air into oxygen-deprived lungs. They stared at each other.

Needing to stop the tiptoeing around their obvious attraction for each other, he cocked his head, and asked in as calm a voice as he could muster, "Well, Lucy? Where do we go from here? It's your decision."

At this moment, her answer was the most important response in his entire life. Right now he didn't give a damn about Farelli, or stolen money, or even the luxury sports car waiting downstairs. He needed to get Lucy out of his system once and for all.

The only problem was, when she reached down, grasped

the bottom of her sweatshirt, and pulled it over her head, Jake didn't know if what they were about to do was going to ease his obsession with her, or make it even stronger.

He feared he already knew the answer.

Chapter Eleven

Lucy dropped her sweatshirt to the floor and stared into Jake's eyes, unsure of what she was doing. It was a step she couldn't take back, didn't want to take back, but still she hesitated. She knew she was already emotionally invested in him, but she wasn't sure about his feelings for her.

He'd told her he was sorry for involving her. That was all well and good, but it didn't tell her how he felt. That he might want her beyond the present. Beyond the extremity of their current circumstances. And without that knowledge, she was running the risk of injuring her heart. But she already knew she wouldn't change her mind. She needed to experience taking Jake Dalton. Being taken by Jake Dalton. She'd deal with her emotions later.

Mind made up, she focused on him once more. He looked dazed, though his eyes kept bouncing down to her breasts and then back to her face.

His tongue came out to lick his lips. And then his hands

came to rest on her hips. He drew her to him, where she couldn't mistake what her topless state did to him.

"Shit, Lucy," he whispered, his warm breath fanning over her like an erotic breeze. She nearly sighed from the feel of him against her, around her. It was like coming home. But he was still talking. "Are you sure? I hope to God you are, but…are you sure this is what you want?"

Taking great care, she looped her arms around his neck as an answer. Squashed her breasts against his chest and, before she changed her mind, rasped, "I want you, Jake. Before you go off to who knows what, I want to be with you. Now. I think I deserve that much."

His hands left her waist. He wrapped his arms around her, tight, and buried his face in her hair. "I didn't lie when I said a moment ago that I wish like hell I hadn't involved you in my mess of a life. That you hadn't been hurt because of me. But this?" He raked her up and down with hot eyes that left little thrills of anticipation along her skin. "You giving yourself to me? Wanting me? I don't regret for one minute. Won't regret."

She marveled at his declaration. Here she was, thrown together, going on twenty-four hours without sleep, and his words made her feel like Cinderella: beautiful and perfect and just a little sexy. Well, maybe a lot sexy, judging by the evidence of his desire she'd felt when he held her tight against him.

He'd seen her at her worst, she'd definitely seen him at his, and yet this…attraction had grown between them. Maybe she was just a sucker for lost causes, that was her usual MO, after all, but this thing between her and Jake? It was mutual, and she wasn't about to lose this opportunity to show him exactly how she felt. She'd raised herself, put herself through school, and gotten the job she'd worked for. It was time she got the man she wanted too.

"I won't regret this, Jake," she said, dragging him back to her. "I want you, and you want me. Isn't that enough for now?"

He tilted her chin up, smiled down at her. "I'm going to try like hell to make it never enough, Lucy. And we're going to love every minute of it. Starting now." He rocked his hips forward, brushed her with that part of him that corroborated his assertion. Grinned wider as she blinked. And then at last, he lowered his mouth to hers.

It was just like the first time. When Jake's calloused hands came up to frame her face and held it steady while he plundered her waiting mouth, Lucy lost all ability to think, and just *felt*.

His lips controlled the kiss, moved over hers with a surety and passion that burned her at their point of contact. She felt so hot she thought she would melt right into his body.

"Christ," he bleated, stumbling backward. He grabbed her hips and tugged at her jeans. Sensing his urgency, she whipped the offending garment down her legs, kicked it off along with her shoes while leaving on the snippet of purple lace panties.

He groaned aloud, snatched her body close once more. She wrapped her arms and legs around him, wiggled against the straining front of his jeans as she tried to hide her smile of satisfaction. She was driving him crazy. The knowledge armed her with a power she'd never known she possessed.

And then he switched it up.

With his fingers digging into the flesh of her bottom, he lowered his head to her breasts, breathed deep and squeezed her closer against his hardened body. He twirled them both around and she couldn't help but squeal at the dizziness. Her squeals ended in a squawk of surprise when he fell backward onto the king-size bed, taking her with him.

As soon as the bed stopped bouncing—and damn, he wished it wouldn't stop bouncing—he rolled Lucy under him and then paused, met her suddenly serious gaze. He realized he needed to lose his Neanderthal tendencies and slow this train down. See where it was going if they made this decision. Of course, she'd given him the go-ahead by taking off her clothes. And he already understood that sex with her would be like the woman herself: complex and unforgettable. But was it the right thing to do?

He was hot for her bombshell body. That was a given. Had been since he'd met her. But beyond the physical, he was attracted to her mind, to her sense of humor. To her independence. To her insecurities. She was unlike any woman he'd ever been with before and he didn't want to screw up what they had, what they'd started.

And it was that last part that really worried him. It meant that he was getting in over his head, and Jake didn't do that. He was a cop first, a man second. Until he turned in his badge, his life didn't have room in it for a long-haired, glasses-wearing accountant who made him think beyond the present. At least, that's what he'd figured up to now. Shit, he felt like a contestant on *Let's Make a Deal*, facing three doors he didn't know how to choose between.

"This is it, sweetheart," he said, searching her face. "There's no turning back. So speak now, or prepare for the ride of your life. I'm not bragging, either. It's a statement of fact." He owed her one last chance to change her mind, though he hoped like hell she wanted him as much as he wanted her.

While he lay atop her as still as a wax statue, she smiled at him with sooty eyes. "I'm not changing my mind. Ride me."

Well damn him to hell. He'd never had a woman tell him to "ride me." Never. Here he'd been worrying so much about her lack of self-confidence, and then she said something like that. He felt himself stiffen even more and decided he'd seesawed long enough. Lucy was a big girl and knew what she wanted. And it was the same thing he wanted.

He stood and shucked his underwear, then joined her amongst the scattered pillows. Centered himself between her upright knees and looked down into her bespectacled, flushed-with-passion face. Gently, for now he had all the time in the world, he reached up and carefully removed her glasses and placed them on the bedside table.

"You won't need to see very far, sweetheart. All our work is gonna be done up close," he whispered. As he gazed down at her, he saw desire, yes, and also trust. Trust that, as she gave herself to him, he would do right by her. And he vowed then and there to be all he could be for her today. Today and forever, for as long as they had. He lowered his mouth to hers to make good on that silent promise.

Tamping down his eagerness, he gently pulled her lower lip into his mouth, sucked on it with a grazing of teeth, and was rewarded with a purely Lucy whimper and sexy squirm. Pleased with her reaction, he repeated the act. Her unique fragrance and softness enveloped him.

He nibbled down her throat, goaded on by her legs wrapping around his hips and pinning him to her body. Oh, yeah, it was about to speed up now. She didn't want to take it slow any more than he did. She was his perfect match, in tune with his thoughts and his needs.

Using his tongue, he cruised down between those lace-covered mounds she seemed self-conscious of and, for the life of him, he couldn't imagine why. She was a walking fantasy. Everything he'd imagined wrapped up in the perfect woman.

With two fingers, he expertly flicked open the purple clasp, and freed her magnificent breasts. He rocked against her, watched her eyes widen at the feel of his arousal. "I've been hard like that for as long as I've been around you. I can't remember wanting a woman as much as I want you right now. So give me the real Lucy Parker. Don't hold anything back."

She started to demur. "What are you talking ab—ahh," she interrupted herself as he ignored her objection and lowered his mouth to one of her breasts, took the nipple between his lips and sucked deeply. She gasped and arched into the caress, hands leaving his hair to fist the bedspread as he explored what made her sigh, what made her wriggle. What made her lose her inhibitions.

Moving his mouth to the other breast, he repeated his ministrations, while one hand plucked and rolled the opposite peak. She bucked again, nearly unseating him, and he chuckled against her skin. He let one hand trail down her body, slip into those panties, and tug on them until she helped him pull them off. And then he drifted away from her breast, kissed at her stomach and lower.

"Please," she begged, rolling her head on the pillow, but he just shook his head, while his tongue continued its track down her body. He explored her belly button for precious seconds while sliding his hands under her bottom and squeezing. He wanted to prolong this adventure of discovery, feel her unravel for him.

Once more he was on the move, licking along one leg, nibbling behind a knee, repeating his seductive journey up the other appendage, and making leisurely stops along the way.

Her body undulated, tightening like a bow against that growing demand for completion. Her hands reached blindly for any part of him, urged him to put out the fire he was building within her. His own body ached to claim her, demanded he take her long and hard, but still he teased with lips and tongue and fingers, prolonging the moment. Taunting himself as much as he tormented her.

Finally, because he feared he might not outlast her if he prolonged this sensual assault any longer, he acquiesced to her pleas, placed his mouth where she begged for him to go.

She shattered as soon as he settled in, the second his mouth met her core. As the echoes of her sighs faded in the room, a strange contentment flowed through him though he hadn't yet found his own release. He fought back an idiotic smile, wondered if he could be drunk on her taste. He already wanted to drink his fill again.

He sat back and regarded her from his current position. His response to her climax left him shaken, even as he admired her in this sated state, with limbs all akimbo, like a doll dropped from a child's careless hand. Every once in a while he'd see a finger twitch, a foot jerk.

Not ready to face the ramifications of why he felt so satisfied watching Lucy climax, he crawled up her body. "That hit the spot, I take it?"

Her heavy-lidded gaze and tremulous smile caused a wave of tenderness to wash over him. He had to touch her to reassure both of them that this was real.

With a gentle hand he smoothed her long, damp hair away from her neck and smiled when her lashes fluttered at his delicate touch.

"Are you game for round two?"

She nodded, still drifting along on the current of a well-loved afterglow.

"Then hold that thought, darling, while I go get my limited supply of—"

"I'm on the pill."

In the midst of leaving he froze, brows rising.

"And you brought them?" He wondered at the implication. "I'm clean, just so you know. They test you for all sorts of things in prison. Can't have the scum of the earth catching any nasty diseases, now, can they?" His voice dripped with sudden sarcasm. "But, I can whip one on," he suggested, "if it'll give you peace of mind." Her outstretched arms had him returning to his former position between her legs, face suspended only inches above hers.

"I'm clean, too. And I'm tired of talking." She reached and buried her fingers in his hair.

"Hmm, a woman of action. I like that." He kneed her legs wider apart, settled in. It didn't take a second invitation to have him sliding into her, filling her. But then he froze, stunned at the sensations, by the effect of their joining.

This was Lucy, *his Lucy*, shy and ferocious at times, seductive but reserved, cautious and curious. And they were... one. The thought overwhelmed him. He had never viewed sex this way before.

He'd always considered sex to be a mutually gratifying activity between two like-minded people. A "you scratch my itch and I'll scratch yours" affair. Granted, he'd wanted to nail this particular girl for days. But now that he was about to seal the deal, it didn't feel like "nailing." It felt deeper. Almost spiritual. A returning home to what was right. He shied away from the implications of that thought.

He rocked forward and backward, slowly, reverently. He wanted to savor the experience of her surrounding him, overpowering him. Drown in her very presence.

But his body had other ideas. Already he could feel the tingle of his climax pulsing at the base of his spine. With each thrust into her tight heat, he inched closer to the edge. He'd lusted after her for far too long, and now she was going to pay the price. Sonofabitch. He hadn't had such lack of control since his teenage years. But then, he couldn't remember ever wanting a girl, a *woman*, as much as he wanted Lucy.

Her hands dove into his hair and she cried out, giving him hope that he wasn't going to leave her in the dust. He dug deep and found the strength, the self-discipline, to back off his own selfish mission, to slow down the force of his thrusts that were inelegantly scooting them across the bed. His heartbeat buzzed in his ears, and he lowered his mouth to hers, took a frantic kiss before reaching between their joined bodies. He stroked her, teased her with nimble fingers until his name flowed off her lips in a breathless keen.

Only then, when he knew she pulsed and shuddered, could he let himself go. With one last powerful thrust, the orgasm plowed over him, thundered through his body. Jake shouted his release, collapsing on top of Lucy after he'd spent himself completely within her.

She subsided against him, panting, arms loosely twined around his neck. His whole being shook. He was stunned at his reaction. It went beyond anything he'd ever experienced and he found he didn't want to break their physical connection. He floated down from that glorious, sensual high with a curious sense of loss, a sadness that he couldn't keep giving her, them, that excruciating pleasure, forever.

Although she hadn't complained about his deadweight, he rolled to his side. Pulled her against him snugly while his chest heaved like a bellows in the aftermath. With eyes tightly clenched, he ran trembling fingers through her hair.

Holy, holy shit. He'd known sex would be good with Lucy. Their mutual attraction had been the guarantee. But hell, it hadn't been good. It hadn't even been great. Having sex with Lucy, making love to her, had been mind-altering. *Mind-blowing*. He hadn't expected quite that intense an outcome.

So when one of her hands found its way to his chest and rested over his heart, he clasped it with his free hand, brought it to his lips. She sighed, long and deep while burrowing into his body.

He'd seriously underestimated the power of their union. He didn't think he'd ever be the same again.

So, Nicky Costas, aka Jake Dalton, had headed for Vegas in a fancy sports car with the plus-size babe from the apartment riding shotgun. *Now what did they plan to do there?* Michael thought as he disconnected the call from the tail he'd put on the undercover cop.

He'd been surprised, no, *stunned*, when he'd found out Costas was really Dalton's undercover persona. He could even admit his hands had been shaking on the keyboard as he'd stared at the proof. It had taken him a while to ferret out the information, given the back door avenues he'd had to travel. But he was certainly glad he'd persevered.

And then there was Tommy, also known as Jerry Litton, another freaking cop. Hell, there were more badges in the Farelli organization than drug dealers. And here he sat, perched on the edge of disaster, his own lucrative side business in danger of exposure.

As much as he hated to admit it, Michael knew when it was time to fold. Now that Farelli realized he'd been ripped off, he would be more vigilant. No, this gig had definitely run its course.

Moving to his laptop, he keyed in his offshore account, checked its balance. Satisfied that all was as it should be, he logged off and stared into space. Why was Dalton going to Vegas? It couldn't be for any good reason. That's why he'd told his man to keep tailing the undercover cop and his bimbo. Michael guessed it had something to do with him, even though he was always careful to cover his tracks. Something had caught Dalton's interest and he wouldn't rest until he was satisfied.

Well, Michael would just have to go and find out what Dalton thought he'd found. Waking up the computer, he bought an airline ticket to Vegas. Jake Dalton had become a problem that needed to be silenced once and for all.

Too bad he hadn't been able to kidnap the girl back at her apartment. No, scratch that. Too bad he hadn't known Nicky was really a *cop* until now. He'd broken into the bitch's apartment to use her as leverage, to get Nicky to tell him where the hidden money was.

If he'd known Nicky was Dalton he would have gone about it all differently. Chosen a more lawful route, though he probably still would have taken the girl. Letting Jake know what was going to happen to her while he was arrested for being a dirty cop would have been sweet retribution.

Ah, well, now that he had found out Jake's little secret, he had to follow the next logical path. Which was to tie up loose ends. And once that was done, he'd cut his losses and get the hell out of the country. He had a safe place already waiting.

The last thing he did was shut down his computer before packing it in his bag. He didn't even blink as the official US government login screen flashed off. He'd been looking at it for too many years.

Chapter Twelve

Jake woke abruptly, the daylight streaming in through the floor-to-ceiling windows too bright for his sleep-heavy eyes. Turning his head to the side, he took in the rumpled, unfamiliar comforter, pillows tossed negligently to the floor, and his own nudity.

At the sound of running water in the adjacent bathroom, he sat up. The morning and previous night all came crashing back to him. Mainly this morning, when he'd finally gotten Lucy naked and screaming under him. Oh, yeah, there was the reason for the torn up bed and the new erection. Damn, but she had been hot. Everything he'd imagined and more.

He fell back onto the bed, ignoring his aroused state and attempted to block the picture of a bare-bottomed Lucy standing under a steamy showerhead. He hadn't gotten enough of her and he'd wasted nearly five hours of prime make-out time snoozing the day away. Shit, old men preferred sleep over sex. He used to be a marathon man in the bedroom Olympics. Now he was spending more time *thinking* about screwing her, instead of actually *doing* her.

But before he went in search of little Lucy all sopping wet, an image from earlier crowded his brain, demanded he peruse it no matter how much he wanted to ignore it. He couldn't forget when, after all the shouting had been done, he'd collapsed on the bed and pulled panting, spent Lucy toward him. How she'd curled into him and pressed her palm against his heart. He couldn't overlook that then, and only then, had he been able to fall asleep.

Glancing at the closed bathroom door, his heartbeat sped up at the thought of being with her again. He paused, pondered the importance of his racing pulse.

He rested against the pillows and closed his eyes, picturing his life without the danger, without the running. Without Lucy. And his heart nearly stopped. Forget that it had felt so right living with her, cooking for her, seeing her at the end of the day. Looking forward to her company. Jake's life was a freaking mess right now and becoming emotionally dependent on Lucy would only compound his problems.

He should get up, quietly dress, and leave. Walk away from Lucy Parker and all the turmoil she provoked within him. He should take care of his chaotic life and let her return to her orderly one. Yes, that would be the wisest move.

He even got out of bed, intent on following that decision. Actually reached for his boxers on the floor. But then he glanced toward the bathroom one more time and saw Lucy in his mind's eye, Lucy with her small hands caressing his skin, her body pressed against his as if they could become one simply by touch. And he damned his heart as he veered toward the bathroom like a magnet.

He threw the bathroom door open. Lucy turned around under the steaming waterfall. She met his gaze and smiled.

He was a goner. With that pleading, big-eyed expression, and water cascading over wet shoulders and off glistening breasts, she beckoned him to dive in and hold nothing back.

But no, he wouldn't go there. Jake Dalton didn't say the L-word, let alone act on it. He shoved the sentiment to the back of his mind, locked the door, and threw away the key.

She held out her hand in invitation, equal parts seductive and insecure. And it was that wide-eyed look that finished him off. That hint of vulnerability that made him want to sweep her up and hold her close. Stepping into the shower and closing the glass door, he maneuvered her up against the cold, white tiles. He felt her body jolt at the chilly contact as he pressed her entire front against his.

"Mmm," he growled, trapping her with his body and placing both hands on either side of her head. She raised her chin, lashes spiked from the flowing water. And still said nothing.

He leaned in, lips just inches above hers. "What's the matter, sweet Lucy? Having second thoughts?"

She shook her head, her gaze dropping to his mouth. She shivered even though the water dousing them remained warm and steady. Rivulets coursed through his hair, dripped off the ends to mingle with the water running over her body. Droplets gummed his lashes, trickled from his nose. He searched for a reason for her reticence.

Pressing closer, he felt her every curve. "Remember, no regrets. I've wanted you since I met you. That's not gonna change. Let's see where this wave takes us." The door in his mind crept open even without the key, but he slammed it, shutting out that traitorous, four-letter word. Instead, he closed the distance between their mouths and captured her lips.

His tongue explored, licked the moisture from her lips before sinking into a long, slow kiss that drugged his senses and dizzied his brain. Once more she was surrounding him, crowding him, muddling his emotions. Unlocking that door…

She pressed her breasts into his chest and wrapped one leg around one of his. He angled his hips and pushed inside her.

For the third time in the last six hours, he lost all sense of time and place, didn't know up from down. He nearly shouted his frustration at his inability to keep this strictly sexual. She had some hold over him, some ability to worm past his defenses, until all he could do was give himself over to her and hope she left something of him at the end.

Oh, God, Lucy screamed in her head as Jake lifted and lowered her body, immediately striking a rhythm. She barely heard his comment of "no regrets." There would always be regrets, but she shoved them aside. She wanted—no, *needed* this man, his touch, his kiss, his body.

His thrusts strengthened, sending her up the shower wall. Over and over he plunged into her, harder, faster, almost as if something was driving him. She clung to him, thoughts careening around in her head until that familiar, swirling need began to build within her.

And then, all at once, his wild, primitive pace slowed,

gentled, becoming long strokes that built the pressure within her even more rapidly. Just when she thought she couldn't take anymore, the coil of tension released, and she bit his shoulder to keep from crying out. Wave after wave of pleasure washed over her, even as she felt him shudder deep inside. She could hear the sound of their labored breathing above the rush of warm shower water while it continued to pelt their entwined bodies.

At last he lowered her to her feet and she wrapped her arms tightly about his waist, heard his wildly-beating heart beneath her ear. She jerked when he rained whisper-soft kisses along the crown of her head. And knew her feelings for him had just gone deeper. No longer was it just a matter of needing him, wanting him. It was now a matter of love…

When the water grew cool, she felt him reach out and turn the water off. She didn't want to move from this place. She wanted to remain in his arms where she felt safe.

He pushed the glass door open and startled her out of her self-examination when he swept her up into his arms and deposited her on the waiting bath mat.

She remained where he'd put her, dazed by her newly uncovered emotions. No man had ever made her feel the way she had moments ago, the way she still felt. That she wasn't complete without him. That her needs and desires were more important than his. That his happiness hinged on hers.

Their gazes collided as he reached for a towel, and he smiled gently. He even winked, before surprising her further by drying her off. He rubbed the towel over her, spending long, sensuous minutes over and between her breasts, around her buttocks, and along her legs.

She was weak-kneed by the time he finished. Ignoring his own wet body, he put the towel to her hair, blotting it while he stood so close she could see the individual water droplets on his chest.

She fought the urge to reach out, to lick the moisture from his skin, and perhaps incite another round of lovemaking. It wouldn't be smart, not when she was so vulnerable from their last coupling. She settled for wrapping her arms around his slim waist, nestling into his damp body, and acknowledging that she'd already lost her heart to this man. That he'd made her love him by everything he said, everything he did. Which only complicated an already difficult situation.

"I still have to go to that gas station on the other end of the Strip, sweetheart." His voice rumbled above her, and he shocked her once again when he dropped the towel and began to run his fingers through her long hair, separating and smoothing out the tangles. Oh, God, she felt like purring, and tightened her embrace. He grunted as his body reacted to her hug.

"Don't get me wrong," he began. "I'd much rather stay here with you—"

Lucy pressed the palms of her hands into his chest and pushed away from him. The erotic moment, that flash of self-discovery, evaporated as his words sank in

"Wait a minute. Even after all we've done, you're planning on leaving me here while you go investigate who's setting you up? Did I hear you right?"

He had the grace to look away, the rat, which told her all she needed to know. Grabbing the towel, she hastily wrapped it around her before meeting his eyes with a glare.

"What am I supposed to do while you're out detecting?

Go get my nails done? Play the slots? I'm good enough to screw, but not good enough to include in your little fact-finding mission?"

Her anger sparked, Lucy stomped out of the bathroom. The rustle behind her announced that Jake was on the move as well. She'd made it to the step down in the other room before he grabbed her elbow and swung her around.

"Stop it, Luce. Just stop and listen for a second."

She shook her arm free and glared at him. Hadn't they just been in this position a few hours ago? Not much had changed — yet everything was different. Against her better judgment, Jake was becoming too important to her. She was falling for his special blend of strength and need. She could only hope he was doing the same for her. But it didn't sound like it.

"I'm going with you, Jake."

"Damn it, Lucy," he whispered. "It's dangerous. I don't want you involved any more than you already are."

She felt him cracking, could hear it in his voice. And she squelched the flood of satisfaction as it rushed through her.

"You may not want me along, Jake, but you can't control what I do. What I feel. I need to be with you. Finding the real person behind all this matters just as much to me as it does to you."

At last he reacted by reaching up and framing her face with his two large hands. He glowered at her. "Why, Lucy? After all I've put you through, exposed you to, why would what affects me matter to you?"

"Because you matter to me, Jake." As an accountant she was a numbers girl, and there was a likelihood that their time was limited. She wouldn't squander it because of her fears or insecurities. Jake deserved more than that—they both did. "I'm involved, whether you like it or not. Wouldn't the safest place for me be with you?"

After a long, tension-filled moment, he acquiesced, yanking her to him, where she could feel his hot skin, feel what her nearness did to him. He swayed from foot to foot, holding her tight. And she felt safe.

"Damn you, Lucy. I can't say no. But you'd better do what I say."

As she rose up on tiptoes to kiss his grudging lips, she whispered, "Yes, dear." He snorted as he lowered his head.

Chapter Thirteen

They drove out to the gas station a little later than Jake had planned, but he wasn't complaining. How could he, when he was so sated from the nonstop lovemaking?

But what made their time together even more special had been the moments in between lovemaking. The times when, sprawled across his body, she'd admitted that her early years had been painful, that she'd had no one to rely on but herself. It had cut him to the quick to visualize a teenage Lucy, coming home to a drunken mother and having to earn the money to keep a roof over their heads and food in their stomachs. He'd told her that her past had made her the strong, captivating woman he admired today. And he'd meant it.

In return, she had held him close when he'd disclosed the facts about his druggie dad, his overworked mom. She'd said she understood now why these accusations weighed so heavily upon him. That he wanted to be nothing like his father. She really got it.

Once they'd turned into the gas station and parked, Jake didn't tell Lucy to wait in the car. She wanted to be with him every step of the way, and why not? He could keep her safer if she was right under his nose. Besides, he was beginning to feel incomplete without her by his side. But he refused to analyze the reason why.

As she came around to his side of the car, it warmed him to realize that he knew each delicious curve and hollow she hid beneath that bulky sweatshirt. That he'd touched and kissed every part of her that she concealed from the outside world. And even more than the sex, he was privy to her secret insecurities, and she of his. He'd never been the recipient of that kind of…whatever you called it.

Avoiding any sort of introspection, Jake turned his attention to the moment at hand. To the clue that could clear his name as a dirty cop.

"How are you going to get the video tape for a particular day?" Lucy asked as she rounded the hood of the car. "They're not going to just give it to you because you asked."

Ah, smart women. Gotta love 'em.

Taking her elbow, Jake ambled toward the cashier inside the station.

"I know that. I've got my story all thought out. Just watch and stay mute. If you can." He intercepted her narrow-eyed look and grinned, then opened the glass door and let her precede him inside. The smell of hot dogs assailed them as they entered.

Luckily, the clerk wasn't with a customer at the moment. She looked up from slurping her Big Gulp and asked in a nasally tone, "Can I help you?"

Jake dragged his attention from the nose ring the girl sported and smiled the smile he reserved for picking up girls. Lucy wandered over to the candy rack, but he knew she was listening.

Leaning on the counter, he read the clerk's nametag. "I sure hope so…Candy, is it? A week ago I was in a fender bender out there in your driveway, and I was hoping your video cameras caught it on tape. Is there any way I could review your video feed?"

She blew a bubble, popped it, chewed it back into her mouth, and shrugged.

"I dunno how to work the video. Sid does that. He's off today—"

"Oh, I know how, Candy. I'm a music scout for some of the casinos. I can run it back without a bit of trouble to you." He saw Lucy's gaze shoot to him in disbelief, but he ignored her. Instead, he held his breath, forced the smile to remain on his face while he chanted within, *C'mon girl, be lazy. C'mon…*

"Sure, why not? It's not like you're gonna steal anything, right?" While she spoke, Candy lifted the split counter, and Jake slid in with a relieved sigh. Lucy positioned herself on the other side so that she could see the video screen. She kept quiet.

More customers filtered in, and the clerk got busy, so Jake did too. Deftly he hit the rewind, and watched the week back up in hyper speed. His captain hadn't given him a definite date of when the money passed here, but he had an approximate. He'd find it. He had to. He just hoped he would recognize one of the guilty persons on the surveillance feed.

Time passed. He felt the tension mounting within Lucy

from across the counter, even though she never spoke, never touched him. He was so in tune with her he could feel her mood as she hovered on the edge of his periphery. He steered his attention back to the camera. The screen was bisected into quarters, with different angles of the inside and outside of the store. He focused on the cash registers.

He almost missed the transaction it was so quick. But there was something about the tilt of the guy's head in the video as he approached the counter and handed the clerk money for gas. It caught Jake's interest, made him pause the tape. He stared at the back of the customer, the way he stood, and felt sweat break out over his body. Those tingles that never failed to warn him he was onto a hot lead began coursing through him. Leaning forward, he alternated between play and pause, slowing the video down frame by frame, until the dude turned to leave. And that's when he recognized the man.

"Well, I'll be damned," he muttered as he watched Michael Delano finish paying and walk in slo-mo out of view on the video.

"I know that guy," Lucy said, startling Jake by her sudden speech. He whipped around to look at her. She nodded. "Yeah. He was at my complex the day of the break in. He was looking for his grandmother's apartment." She raised her gaze to his. "You don't think —"

"That's exactly what I think," Jake said, pushing the eject button and snatching out the disc. He handed it off to Lucy, fished out two one hundred-dollar bills, and tossed them at Candy, backing up as he did so.

"Thanks a lot, Candy. I found what I need. Keep a hundred for yourself, and tell Sid to use the other for a new disc.

I need this one." Grabbing Lucy's elbow, he dragged her out of the little gas station store, towing her all the way to the Porsche amidst Candy's indignant calls for him to stop.

He wouldn't answer Lucy's insistent questions until he'd put the car in gear and merged onto Las Vegas Boulevard. Only then did he slow his careening mind enough to say, "You met that guy where you lived? Right before we were attacked? And you never mentioned it?" He couldn't control his rising voice. Shit, all this time the answer was sitting in Lucy's brain and he hadn't known it?

Apparently, his tone had been too strident, for Lucy slouched in the bucket seat, arms crossed over those luscious breasts he'd— *Down boy. You're irritated with her, remember?*

"It slipped my mind, all right? He was just looking for one of my neighbors. It wasn't any big deal. Who is he, anyway?"

Zipping between a bus and a lumbering SUV, Jake shot her a glance. "Only Farelli's right hand man. Michael "Dickweed" Delano. The guy I also suspect might be a cop."

Michael threw his phone across the room in a moment of childish anger. He'd just gotten news from the tail that the cop and his girlfriend had paid a visit to a gas station Michael frequented.

The news pissed him off. What the hell did that stupid bloodhound think he could find out there? He was too good to get caught by some wannabe detective. He'd been playing both sides for too long to be brought down by the likes of

Dalton.

He stared out the window at the gaudy Strip, not really seeing it. Instead, he was remembering when he'd first obtained entrance into Farelli's private circle, investigating the drug operation as Michael Delano. Anton Farelli's right hand man and general clean up committee of one. And he'd certainly been cleaning up, monetarily speaking, ever since.

Absently running a hand over his short hair, he recalled the first time he took payment from Farelli and squirreled some of it away in a secret account, with no plan of handing it over to his boss, Uncle Sam. He'd been sick to his stomach with fear of getting caught.

But as the days went by and more payments were received and stockpiled without issue, he found it easier and easier to make half his remuneration just "disappear." His reports to the Feds hadn't changed. Only the amounts. And now here he was. A Rolex watch on his wrist, an Audi in the garage below, and Armani suits in his penthouse closet.

Confirming the hour on said timepiece, he turned from the lights and glitz before him and glanced about the room, remembering how he'd always managed to keep his superiors from getting suspicious of his lucrative double life. He had learned how to feed them a few fish every once in a while to keep them happy and content that he was doing his job, while he still maintained his new standard of living.

And when they sent him some "help" to get the job done faster, why, that person always found a sad ending to his life, with the excuse that the poor sap had been found out. *He* was the only one to have gotten close enough to Farelli to gain his trust and he was determined to keep it that way. Right now it was a win-win situation for everyone concerned. No two-bit cop from San Bernardino was going to change that fact.

Sitting back down on the bed, Michael pondered what Dalton could be hunting for at the gas station. His snitch had said the cop had been booking it to his car. That meant he thought he had something.

Michael glanced out the window one more time. He should just jump a plane. He didn't owe Farelli anything, or the FBI. Hell, he knew how to hide. No one would ever find him if he didn't want them to.

But Dalton was handing him the perfect chance to blame it all on him. If he intercepted the girl and Dalton, killed them, and then told Farelli they had admitted to skimming his money, why, he might be able to maintain his position just a little longer. It all depended on what Dalton had discovered. Otherwise, he'd still kill them and disappear. Worked for him.

Now that he had a game plan, all he had to do was snap the ball. And no better time than the present. He'd just go over and pay Dalton a little visit. A dropped hundred here or there worked wonders in the information business. Maybe he'd even have a little fun with Dalton's plump companion. Give her something to remember before she died.

When they got back to the hotel, Jake hustled them both straight to the suite, where, luckily, housekeeping had tidied the room. Lucy felt a blush start up her neck and face just from looking at the bed, and new tingles began low in her body. She should be exhausted. She should be scared.

She shouldn't be thinking about taking her clothes off, or removing Jake's. But then, she'd already concluded that she was a goner for the guy.

As soon as the door shut behind him, Jake leaned back against it. "I can't believe you didn't think a chance meeting with a strange guy didn't warrant letting me know. Especially after I kidnapped you."

Those sensual tingles evaporated and Lucy pivoted, got right up into his face. She was tired, and tired of being reamed out. All she wanted was to be held. "That's why I didn't mention it. Because at the time, you were the only one who posed a danger to me and you were in my house."

They glared at each other until he suddenly opened his arms and invited her in. She moved without hesitation, snuggling against him as he said over her head, "Point taken. But you should have remembered after the attack." This last he said without bite, though, so Lucy didn't reply. It felt too good in his embrace to risk leaving it for another pointless argument.

"What did you mean, you think this guy's a cop?" she asked instead.

"Just that. When I Googled him, his public info read like mine. Or rather, like Nicky's. Too bland. Too pat. But I couldn't use my official capacity to dig deeper. I didn't want anyone knowing where I was or what I was looking up. But now I can have my captain dig up the dirt on Delano. So I have to call him."

"It's almost over, isn't it?" She held tight to his waist. He nodded, and she saw that look she recognized, that look that said he wanted to kiss her. And she wanted him to. But her stomach took that moment to growl, long and loud, and she wished the floor would open up and swallow her. How embarrassing. But she couldn't remember the last time she'd eaten anything. They'd been on the go since the break-in.

Jake raised his brows, and the moment was gone. He gave her a quick peck on the forehead and moved toward the phone. "After I call the captain, we'll get room service, and then pick up where we left off. The bathroom, right?" He delivered that sexy smirk that melted her insides. She nodded mutely, while he dialed out on the hotel phone.

Her stomach continued its complaining while Jake contacted his commanding officer. Lucy grabbed some pretzels off the snack tray while Jake argued over Delano's importance. He must have gotten his point across, for pretty soon he was nodding and saying, "yeah" at regular intervals, as if his captain was reading something to him.

This discussion could go on forever. Lucy sighed, polishing off the meager snack. Casting one more look at Jake, who was now sitting by the phone with his back to her, she decided she was done waiting. She could zip right down to one of the restaurants in the casino, order some food, and bring it back. Once she shut up her stomach, they could move on to dessert. Her body quivered at the thought. She tapped him on the shoulder and whispered, "I'm going to get us food."

He frowned, but then his captain said something and his attention diverted. Lucy took the moment to leave. The room door shut with a click behind her. She headed to the elevator and caught one immediately. While it made its way down to the casino level, she contemplated the idea that she had fallen in love with Jake Dalton.

It was a new feeling for her. Growing up the way she

had, with the parent she had, Lucy had steered clear of emotional entanglements. She'd been too afraid of being a replica of her mother. Oh yes, she'd dated and, if she was honest, she'd probably handpicked her boyfriends for their faults — because that meant she'd never trust them fully, never fall for them so wholeheartedly that she lost a little bit of herself. Love had never factored into the equation. Until now.

The chime of the elevator woke her from her introspection, and she exited into the main casino. Although it was a weekday, the cacophony of slots flooded her ears. Bright, flashing lights, clouds of hovering smoke, and video screens advertising upcoming hotel entertainment accosted her. Vegas never slept.

She headed to the sandwich shop on the outskirts of the casino floor where its to-go line meandered amidst new flooring installation and an equally new wishing fountain. Two sub sandwiches would go a long way toward sating their appetites. Of course, there were other people wanting the same thing so, while she waited her turn, her mind roved from thoughts of loving Jake (she could actually say it in her head now) to worrying over what was going to happen to him now that this case was nearing its end.

Moving up in the queue, she studied the wishing fountain (like Vegas needed to take more money from already spendthrifty tourists), and wondered if Jake's captain was actually listening to him, or just trying to trace the call. They did that in real life and not just in the movies, didn't they? And if he was hearing Jake out, how would he help Jake? There was a hit on him!

"Can I help you, miss?" The clerk's perky question dragged her back into the present. She gave her order before resuming her contemplation, though the construction hammering behind her sounded like it was in her head. Or maybe that was the hunger and worry over Jake's predicament.

Jake faced stiff odds against walking away from this state of affairs, and Lucy's stomach clenched at the thought of him getting shot by Farelli or arrested for being a dirty cop. Death or incarceration. There was really no choice at all. And it all hinged on whether his captain believed him and sent help, or if Jake and she became an army of two to bring down Farelli on their own. Definitely lousy odds. Receiving her order, Lucy picked it up and made her way through the maze of caution tape and cones.

Glancing about, she decided to pop into the nearby restroom. That tinkling fountain reminded her she'd left the room upstairs without doing so. The glitzy gold door she shoved open revealed a restroom that looked like it had undergone a recent reno as well, with its gilt mirrors and shiny marble floor. She was its only inhabitant, seeing as it was tucked behind all the construction going on outside its doors. Once she set the take-out containers on the anteroom's counter, she hustled into the quiet bathroom, glad to be somewhere without a throng of people and noise.

She assessed her appearance in the mirror and grimaced. She looked like she'd been on the run and without sleep for twenty-four hours. Tucking some hair behind her ear, she headed into a stall.

A moment later she heard the restroom entrance door swoosh open, the sound of footsteps as someone entered. Ah, well. Never alone for long in Vegas. When she reached to open her stall, she paused, cocked her head. The footsteps hadn't continued. There was no running water, no movement to another bathroom compartment. Just silence. But she'd heard someone enter. Hadn't she?

There. Wasn't that an inhaled breath? A shifting of a foot? There *was* someone in here with her. So what were they doing? Lucy puzzled through the meaning of the utter stillness. Until she heard a sound that froze her. The telltale click of the ladies' room main door being locked. From the inside. On the heels of that came a chilling laugh. A *man's* laugh. An icy finger of fear slithered down her spine.

"I know you're in here, sweetheart. Come out, come out, wherever you are."

Chapter Fourteen

The singsong, Jack Nicholson-esque whisper echoed off the marble surround, bubbling more chills throughout Lucy's body. The time for their getaway had run out. This was *the* person who wanted Jake and her dead.

Stuffing a knuckle into her mouth, Lucy soundlessly stepped onto the toilet and hunched over so as not to be seen above or below the stall door. With eyes clenched tight, she cast about for hope, listened for someone, anyone, to try the door and find it locked. She wasn't going to die an ignominious death, slouched over an open toilet with blood dripping from a gunshot wound to her heart, was she? That's not how lowly female accountants died. They died at home, alone, reading lurid romance novels with a comfortable tabby curled in their laps.

This was Vegas, after all. People were everywhere in this city, even in restrooms hidden within construction zones. Weren't they? And there were cameras. Casinos used cameras to spy on gamblers all the time. But did they waste them on secondary restrooms and pass-through walkways?—

Wham!

She nearly fell off her toilet perch when her executioner kicked in the first stall door and announced his findings.

"Empty."

Wham!

"Empty again."

She jumped the second time, nearly biting the knuckle she'd used to silence her need to scream for help. Because it looked like she was on her own. And still he continued kicking in the individual stall doors, the ominous sound ringing like her personal death knell. If she'd had more courage, she might have scampered out of her stall into one he'd already investigated. But she was frozen in place by overpowering fear.

When he finally reached her door and met with resistance from the flimsy lock, all she could do was cower silently, staring at the seam where door met metal jam, and where now a green eye peered through.

"Peek-a-boo, I see you." Belying the childish words the man snapped, "Get your ass out here, bitch."

She began sobbing in earnest now. As she staggered off the seat, it took several tries before her quivering fingers managed to loosen the latch. She pulled the door open and, in one last, foolhardy attempt for freedom, ducked her head and charged her assailant. He grabbed her ponytail, yanked her right off her feet, extracting an agonized squeal of pain and panic.

"Let go, let go! *Help!*—"

Grabbing and twisting her long hair around his hand like

a leash, he snapped her toward him. She screamed again, this time in pure pain, earning a backhand for her noise. A throbbing ache radiated through her face, and she fell limp into his arms. If she couldn't escape, she would at least make it darn hard for him to disappear as well.

"Stand up. If you're not going to use your legs, I might as well shoot you in the kneecaps."

This was not how she wanted to go, so Lucy did as she was told, faced her evil captor on wobbly legs. "You're not going to get away with this," she announced, with barely a tremor in her voice. "Jake's on the phone right now with his captain." A momentary relief coursed through her when he let go of her hair. But her stomach dropped when he withdrew a nasty-looking gun from beneath the casual jacket he wore.

He grinned, drawing his coldly handsome features into a radiant smile guaranteed to attract women like bees to a honey pot. He raised the gun and caressed Lucy's stiff face with its muzzle as he mimed a theatrical shiver. "Oh, dear, I'm positively quaking in my boots. What's that old piece of shoe leather going to do to me from his desk chair in San Bernardino, eh? By the time he gets his fat ass on a plane, both you and your bumbling boyfriend will be distant memories."

Those frosty green eyes flicked over her sweatshirt-clad body and he continued, "I was thinking of a way we could while away the time until your Prince Charming came to your rescue, but now that I get a good look at you, I'm not that interested. You're a little too...*ordinary*, for me. Jesus, lose the extra weight, you clumsy cow. And the Coke bottle glasses. You'd be passably pretty if you took some pride in yourself."

Lucy stared into the hateful brute's face. This killer, this awful, awful man who could snuff her life out in a nanosecond, was lecturing her on how to become more attractive? While waving a deadly weapon in her face? Furious, she lost all self-control and swung her hand back to slap him a good one across his stony face.

He shoved the gun barrel against her head. "Don't even think of it. I don't need you now. Your absence is enough to bring Dalton where I want him, so don't make the mistake of getting on my bad side. I could kill you right now and still obtain the result I'm looking for."

Her anger died as she gazed into the man's dead stare. He would make good on his threat, she was sure of it.

"That's better. Respect me, and things will go a lot easier, Lucy Parker. Now, in a moment we're going to walk right out of here arm-in-arm like a loving couple. Oh, and baby makes three," he snickered, waving his gun. Then he shrugged out of his jacket and folded it over his arm before sliding the muzzle under it, close enough to jab her in the ribs. Lucy did as she was told. After all, she might be the only backup Jake would have.

"I know, I know, there aren't any pictures of him anywhere on the web. Just the same bullshit as my Nicky Costas bio. But maybe you can crosscheck the mugshot of Michael Delano in the federal database." Jake glanced toward the room door through which Lucy had disappeared too long ago for his comfort. Shit, what was she doing, making dinner?

He'd been having the strangest tingles down his spine since the gas station and he never discounted those feelings. They'd served as his alarm system for far too long to be ignored. But a warning about what? He'd found who he thought was a double agent in the Farelli outfit and he already knew he was wanted by the drug dealer and his own people. So why the hell was he feeling those tingles?

"I'll run him, but it'll take a little time, Jake."

"Time is the one thing I don't have. Listen, I'll call you back in five and maybe you'll have some info for me." Jake disconnected and slouched onto the bed. He knew he was right about Delano. His captain had to find a connection. No one covered their tracks completely. No one. But those damn warning tingles were still bothering him. And where the hell was Lucy? He hated waiting.

While he sat cooling his heels, Jake thought back over the time he'd spent with her, especially here in Las Vegas. In this room. Everywhere he looked they'd been, bodies seamlessly entwined, as if they couldn't get close enough.

He'd never been in love before, had never been able to witness it between his parents. Yes, he'd always thought he'd find that special someone to share his life with, who didn't? But he hadn't gone out of his way looking for a mate. Especially not now, when his life was a tangle of epic proportions.

The shrill of the phone startled him, so Jake grabbed up the receiver. "Did you find him?"

"Not a him, Costas. A her. A very plump, juicy her, by my standards. It's nice to finally talk to you, Nicky. Or, should I call you Jake?"

Jake went cold all over as the explanation for those warning tingles at last became clear. The reason Lucy had been gone so long. Michael Delano had caught onto them somehow and was holding her hostage. Jake decided to remain silent until he could control the anger racing through him.

With an audible sigh, the speaker continued, "All right, Jake. As you've probably guessed, I've got something of yours that you might have just realized is missing. It's a rather hefty something, but then, there's no accounting for taste." In the background, Jake heard some muffled sounds, followed by the distinct ring of a slap.

A pinpoint flame of hatred flared in his gut like a pilot light.

"If you hurt her, I'll hunt you down," Jake vowed. "And they'll be looking for pieces of you until the next millennium."

Harsh laughter echoed over the phone. "Listen up, Dalton. I'm calling the shots. I've been your shadow since that clumsy escape maneuver of yours, so give up the theatrics. You'll do what I say, because that buffoon you work for will just be getting off his official ass by the time this whole fiasco is over. And, if you do defy me, well, the girl loses." More muted noise met Jake's ears and then a faint cry of pain, as if the bastard had pinched Lucy or twisted her arm.

"Tell me what you want, Delano," Jake barked, knowing he was the only one who could rescue Lucy. The wanted, almost-out-of-options cop on the run. *He* was her knight in shining armor and he found he *wanted* that role.

With an icy calm cloaking his fury, Jake concentrated on relaxing the various muscles that had constricted at the thought of Lucy in pain. He had to find that tranquil place, that state of composure he entered before a bust so he didn't commit some stupid mistake that got him killed. Only now the stakes were higher, because it wasn't his life he had to protect, it was Lucy's. His Lucy.

"Meet me in the basement of the Sirocco in thirty minutes. And, if you value this piece of ass I'm holding, you'd better come alone, or you won't like what I do to her in retaliation. She won't resemble anything you've ever seen. A half hour."

The connection went dead.

Chest heaving, Jake stared at the dead phone. Delano, Farelli's favorite henchman, came with a reputation. A bad one. He knew the man didn't bluff. Jake could call in backup, hell, he could have Vegas SWAT on the site in under ten minutes. But one misstep, one mistake, and Lucy would suffer for it. No. All he could do was go meet him. Meet him, rescue Lucy, and send the bastard to hell where he belonged.

With his mind presenting and tossing out various scenarios to accomplish those objectives, Jake got ready. He picked up the gun Jerry had left him, which he'd been carrying around like a lifeline to the person he'd once been. Then he rummaged through his backpack and pulled out his own gun. After making sure it was loaded, he stuffed it into his sock, pulled his pant leg over it, and headed out the door. He had a scumbag to kill.

Lucy trembled on a straight-backed chair, hands tied behind her back, in the basement of a hotel, in what looked to be some sort of sports club undergoing renovation. It was probably another attempt by Sin City to squeeze every bit of money out of visitors and locals alike by modernizing, but for now it simply resembled a chaotic construction zone where the workers had left right at quitting time. Table saws, two-by-fours, steel beams, along with various hammers, screw drivers, and nail and staple guns littered the space.

The assassin paced the cement floor across from her. Her eyes followed him, gaze riveted on his weapon. She had no idea when he might use it. He had proven to be unpredictable in the short time of their acquaintance. The side of her face paid testimony to that fact.

"Think he'll come to your rescue? Were you that good in bed?" He turned and faced her, his soulless eyes boring into hers.

She shivered, wanting to scream, "You'll never know," but thought that might sound too much like a challenge. Instead, she replied scornfully, "I know Jake will come, and he'll wipe the floor with you."

Those dead eyes narrowed on her face. She managed not to cringe, holding still as he stared down into her face. Reaching out, he grabbed her chin, angling her face to gaze into it from his height. She glared back at him. Finally, he let go of her, backed up and said lightly, "I think I understand what he sees in you. There's quite a fire burning in you for him, isn't there? Lots of passion, hmm?"

"Love," she said. "Lots of love. Something I doubt you could comprehend."

His eyebrows spiked, and a fleeting smile crossed his face.

"You're right. I don't love. In my line of work, it's a hazard. It can get you killed. However," and here he turned sideways, studying her for long seconds. "However," he repeated, "it works in my favor today. Want to know how?" His tone resembled an eager child's. She refused to reply.

"Of course you do. You just don't want to tell me. You see, Dalton loves you so much that he will run here in the hopes of rescuing you before I kill you. Even if he doesn't love you, he'll play his good ol' boy cop role to perfection. And I'm going to give him his moment of glory, saving you. And then I'll kill you anyway."

No. She couldn't let that happen. Because he was right. Jake was coming for her, but it wouldn't do any good. The madman was going to kill them both. Maybe she could distract him. She had to keep him talking and hope that Jake could use that small advantage to his favor.

"Why do you want to kill Jake so badly? Do you two have a history?" It was a stupid question, but if she could just keep Delano talking, maybe Jake would hear his voice and somehow take the killer by surprise. Right, and "for the cop's next magic trick he'd show up with a cannon and blow this guy's head right off his body!" But it was all she could think of to do.

Delano pursed his lips and nodded to himself, gun muzzle resting against his cheek like a lazy finger.

"Do we have a history?" he repeated contemplatively. "I guess you could call it that. You see, Miss Parker, I've been Farelli's right hand man for years now. I've also been the FBI's deepest undercover operative. Adrian Fisk, at your service. The only one to get this close to Farelli and stay close. Everyone else the feebs sent in managed to meet with…accidents." He laughed uproariously. "Until your boyfriend decided to bumble into my world. He and that greedy partner of his. But I succeeded in throwing most of the blame on Jake. Farelli still thinks Dalton was in cahoots with Tommy and, thanks to that weak bastard, I imagine his department would like a few words with him. Right now Jake's the man everyone wants. And I'm sitting pretty, with money coming in from both sides—"

A rumbling noise came to their ears from the service elevator beyond the plastic curtains. His eyebrows shot up, a joyous, Christmas Day enthusiasm crossing his countenance.

"Here he comes. And right on time. A punctual victim. I appreciate that."

"He's got a gun, Jake!" Lucy screamed. In horror movie slow motion, she watched as Delano turned toward her, raised his gun and snapped off a shot in her direction while bellowing, "Shut the hell up, you interfering bitch!"

As the gunshot reverberated through the empty space, she wailed hysterically, hunching into a ball on the chair, expecting the bullet to rip a hole through her. Biting her lip until she tasted blood, she waited for the explosion within her body, when she would feel her insides splatter against the confines of her mutilated skin.

It took precious seconds before she realized she remained whole. No wounds. No fireball of gut-wrenching pain shooting through her, no last thoughts or prayers before eternal oblivion. Yet she continued to cower, rocking in place while saliva seeped from her mouth and silent sobs wracked her body, the aftereffects of staggering terror.

When she accepted that she was still alive, she lifted her head and stared toward the elevator, the same as Delano/Fisk was doing. The doors of the car slid open and, without warning, Delano/Fisk discharged his gun at it.

The ricocheting bullets echoed throughout the space, and Lucy started crying all over again. Jake hadn't had a chance. He'd been a sitting duck in that death car. He'd come to save her but had been killed, and now it was her turn.

She forced her streaming eyes open, wouldn't face death with them closed. And then she jumped in surprise when a blur of motion came from the direction of the stairs, straight toward Delano, who was advancing on the elevator with his gun pointed at it.

Chapter Fifteen

The action movie gambit worked, Jake thought, reaching the bottom of the stairs just as Delano opened fire on the empty elevator. He leaned against the wall and lifted his Beretta. He couldn't see the double agent from here, but he could see Lucy.

Crouching low, he burst through the plastic drapes that screened off the construction area, homing in on Delano. As soon as he had him in his sight he fired. From the corner of his eye, he noticed Lucy's head turn toward him, but he couldn't spare her an encouraging glance. Her life depended on his single-mindedness.

One of his shots clipped Delano. The asshole staggered and whipped around, murder in his eyes. He looked beyond Jake, raised his gun, and squeezed off a round at Lucy. She screamed, huddling into herself with hands still tied behind her back. She kept screaming as she rocked on the hard chair.

Jake pointed the Beretta at Delano and fired. He couldn't miss at this range. He'd kill the asshole—

It clicked. The clip was empty. Goddamnit! Too late to reach for the other gun. As if in slow motion, he saw Michael grin and pull the trigger. *Oh, shit, Lucy. I'm so damn sorry—*

It clicked just as Jake's had done.

Jake's heart started beating again. The scum-sucker was out of ammo and Jake wasn't about to give him time to reload. He threw his useless Beretta at Delano's head, forcing the killer to duck. And then Jake pulled the other gun from his back.

The bastard jumped into the air and kicked the second gun from Jake's hand. It skidded across the floor. Damn that ninja bullshit! Forgetting the weapon for the moment, Jake lunged at Delano and threw a haymaker that should have snapped Delano's head off his neck, but Michael blocked the hit with his forearm. And then he swung a clenched fist the size of a wrecking ball. Jake ducked and charged, gut-ramming the double agent hard. Delano staggered back a pace, but reached out and put his hands on Jake's shoulders, shoving him away. Then he spun around and kicked Jake in the chin.

Jake's teeth clacked together like castanets. He was lucky he hadn't bit his tongue off from the force of the blow. Pain exploded up his jaw, and he fought not to blackout. He shook his head, which only increased his dizziness. Struggling to keep his eyes open, Jake saw Delano make a run for the loaded Beretta. And he knew Lucy would be the bastard's target. He. Had. To. Get. There. First.

He dove for the agent's legs, tackling him, then lurched to his feet. He had only seconds to snatch up the Beretta, aim, and kill the freaking bastard. Fueled by that knowledge, Jake shouted over his shoulder, "Lucy, drop," as he grabbed up the weapon and spun around. Praying that for once she obeyed without the usual "Why?" response, Jake aimed and rapid-fired like a video game enthusiast attacking zombies.

Pow, pow, pow.

Delano subsided after the first few rounds, his head cracking on the concrete floor. Jake strode toward the downed assassin, gun arm outstretched, finger ready on the trigger. With one quick glance he could see that, yes, Lucy had rocked her chair to the floor when he'd told her to. Good girl.

Toeing the body and satisfied Delano was one of the not-so-dearly departed, he tucked the Beretta into his waistband, then knelt before Lucy, blocking her view while untying her hands.

"Are you okay, sweetheart?" He drew her to her knees once he'd released her, cupping her face and thumbing away the tears that seeped out beneath her glasses. She nodded, immediately throwing herself into his arms and hugging him tightly. Jake cradled her for long minutes.

"Shh," he cooed, rocking her. It was over. Somehow, incredibly, they'd beaten the odds.

"It's over, Lucy-love. We did it."

"I-I thought you were going to d-die, Jake. I th-thought he was g-going to kill you and I couldn't stand the thought."

Aww, hell. Here she'd been near death herself, yet all she'd thought about was him. Did he deserve that type of complete devotion?

"Wouldn't ever happen, Lucy," he said in response, his voice husky. "Now that I've got you, I'm sure as shit not going to check out of this life." He pressed her face against his shoulder. He felt his insides clench at the thought that they still weren't clear of this mess.

He might have saved them from Delano's imminent threat, but he—*they*—wouldn't have a chance together if he didn't clear up his current state of affairs. And he knew without a doubt that, after almost thirty-four years in this world, he'd found someone he didn't want to say good-bye to at the end of the day.

So, he detached her vine-like arms from around him and stepped back regretfully. He grabbed hold of her hands and waited until she looked at him. She hiccupped, and he fought the urge to laugh and hug her tight. "Listen to me. You have to get outta here. It's time I called the cavalry and turned myself in. Right now I'm still suspected of stealing evidence. It'll take a while to hash out."

She lifted her eyes to his. More tears tracked down her face as she slowly shook her head.

"I don't care about that, Jake. I—I love you."

Oh, hell. He snatched her back into his embrace, crushing her against him with the strength of his emotion. She'd told him all he needed to know with those three little words, and he was going to do his damnedest to prove he was worthy of her love. But that still didn't change their current circumstances.

He brushed a kiss on top of her head and set her at arms' length. "I love you too, Luce. But there's going to be a lot of fallout from this mess, and I don't want you a part of it. If they want me, they'll have to leave you alone. That's the only deal I'm making. But I've broken a shitload of laws and rules, and it's gonna take forever to sift through."

Still she hesitated.

"You need to leave, sweetheart—"

And then they heard it. The sound of the freight elevator. Someone had heard the gunshots, probably hotel security. The half-empty Beretta Jerry had supplied was still hidden at the small of Jake's back, while Fisk had fallen on the Glock as well as onto Jake's empty gun. He barely had time to shove Lucy behind him before the plastic curtains parted and Anton Farelli, flanked by bodyguards carrying enough firepower to free a small country, stepped through them.

"Hello, Nicky."

Chapter Sixteen

The drug king looked just as slithery as ever, Jake noted with a sinking feeling. His hair, businessman-gray at the temples, was slicked back from his forehead with enough oil to coat all the choices at a salad bar. His open-necked dress shirt in dove gray displayed gold chains glittering on a spray-tanned chest sprinkled with hair.

He gave the impression of a typical mobster movie character except that the company he kept compensated for his unoriginality. His bodyguards wore black suits while carrying their deadly weapons against their chests. They stared right through Jake.

Farelli passed Jake and Lucy, who pressed up against Jake's back like she wanted to crawl inside him. The warmth of her body reminded him that he had more than just himself to consider in this situation. It was sobering.

The drug lord circled Delano's body, cocking his head. Jake knew he couldn't have heard much, if anything, of their discussion and subsequent blowout, so he bet Farelli was wondering what the hell had gone down between them. He just hoped his former boss wouldn't think it was a falling out between thieves, even if that's what it looked like.

When the older man shrugged and moved away from the corpse without a word, Jake was a little surprised. Delano had worked closely with his boss, yet his death brought no more response beyond mild curiosity? Cold. Farelli was stone cold.

In front of them once more, the mobster motioned with one languid hand and a gun-wielding guard stepped forward, reached past Jake, and grabbed hold of Lucy's arm. Jake controlled the knee-jerk reaction of punching the guy in the face. Schooling his features into what he hoped was an emotionless mask, he stared straight ahead as Lucy stumbled by him.

He knew she was waiting for him to do something, anything to show her he cared, but he couldn't. Wouldn't. Doing so would put a bigger target on her than she already had. If he displayed any concern toward her, Farelli would understand she was important to him and would capitalize on it. Jake couldn't afford that. She meant too much to him. Besides, the drug king was a sadistic bastard.

"Nicky, what the hell happened here?" Farelli stepped forward now, hands in his trouser pockets. Two of his henchmen, who looked like they'd been drinking protein shakes since the womb, took up positions on either side of him. At least Jake's cover identity seemed to be intact, judging by the name the drug lord had called him by.

"Delano was your Judas, boss," he said quickly. "He's been taking from you for a year. I found it out for you. He tried to bribe me so I wouldn't tell. Said he would even give me part of his take if I kept quiet."

Farelli nodded. The lie had come easily to Jake and it seemed to be working. He avoided looking at Lucy while waiting for the drug lord's response. She wasn't a good liar. But he was when the situation warranted it.

Pausing, Farelli leaned into Jake. "Where's the gun?" he asked in a moderate tone.

Jake jutted his chin toward the body. "He fell on it." He was going to lose the Beretta under his shirt, Jake figured. No way would they not eventually search him. It was only a matter of time.

Farelli studied him for a long minute. Christ, the silence was killing him. Though he made sure his outward expression didn't change. Glancing down, the older man began twisting a flashy ring upon his little finger. Jake had to bite the inside of his jaw to keep from saying anything.

"I don't believe your story." Without any other warning than that, Farelli backhanded Jake across his face, his gold and diamond signet ring cutting open a good chunk of his cheek in the process. In the split second before the pain hit, he heard Lucy stifle a cry.

"Aargh," Jake exclaimed as his head nearly did that Linda Blair/*Exorcist* thing. He started to reach toward his face, but one of the guards grabbed him by the elbows and pulled them behind him. Blood trickled from his cheek and onto the concrete floor. Head bowed, vision blurring from tears of pain, Jake stared at the widening puddle for a long moment before looking up once more.

Farelli strolled away from Jake while his men ranged themselves around the space, guns at the ready. Jake sucked in deep breaths, willing the pain away, leaning forward as the drug lord spoke in an undertone.

"That's a good story, Nicky. But you know what I think happened? I think it was a disagreement between two pumped up shits who had been stealing from their boss. I think one of you wanted a bigger part of the take, and this is the result of that argument. I took both of you in, all three of you, counting Tommy, trained you in lucrative positions, and the three of you thank me how?"

During his deliberate pause, Farelli pulled out a snowy handkerchief from his inner suit pocket and began wiping Jake's blood off his hand, finger by finger. This took several seconds, during which Jake's heart rate quadrupled in his chest, until Farelli cast a mildly disapproving look at him. "You steal money from me."

Jake shook his head, blood splattering everywhere from his face wound. This was it. If he didn't start tap dancing, the punishment would either be a slow and demoralizing death while he watched them do who-knew-what to Lucy, or a quick double tap to the backs of both their heads. Neither was an outcome he'd choose.

Farelli negligently tossed the used handkerchief at Jake's feet. Jake willed himself to look innocent. He *was* innocent, at least of these accusations. Their gazes held. Moments ticked by. At last Farelli turned away.

Only then did Jake exhale. The pain in his cheek had reduced to a dull throb, though blood still leaked from the wound. But, all in all, he felt fortunate still to be inhaling and exhaling through normal entries and exits. Now he had to convince Farelli he wasn't guilty of skimming the profits.

"I didn't steal from you, boss." As defenses went, it wasn't the best plan. Better to expound a bit. "Tommy acted all on his own. So did Delano. You gotta believe me, Mr. Farelli. You paid me great. I'm not into biting the hand that feeds me—"

"Shut up." Farelli's voice cut across Jake's, and Jake realized that the drug lord had been toying with him this whole time. He was livid.

"Bring the girl here." He snapped his fingers and one of the clowns—Cervantes, Jake recalled from when he worked with them—grabbed Lucy's elbow and dragged her in front of Farelli. A serrated blade of fear cut through Jake, but anger was a close second when he saw the buffoon's gaze drop down to Lucy's breasts. The perv even pulled her closer to his side just to cop a free feel. Jake clenched his fists. He could see Lucy was shaking from head to toe.

Ah, screw this. He couldn't watch them torture Lucy. Not the woman he loved. Anything but that. He swallowed down the hopelessness as it curdled in his stomach. And still wouldn't meet her seeking, trusting gaze.

"I'm done with this shit, Nicky. Tell me where you've hidden the money, or she'll get a cut on her face to match yours. On a man a scar adds mystery. On a woman? It's a disfigurement. Don't take too long to decide. One of you will tell me the truth. I'm giving you the chance to be the gentleman."

Farelli began turning that killer bling on his finger. It was hypnotizing in its evilness. Lucy's head was bowed. Jake looked at that long ponytail, those legs she had wrapped around him in ecstasy. Those arms that drew him into her body, her heart. And he caved without contest.

"I'll tell you where it is, boss. Just leave her alone. She doesn't know anything. I only keep her around for my down time." He saw Lucy's back stiffen. *Ah, sweetheart, please don't shoot off your mouth. I promise, if we get out of this alive, I'll make it up to you. I mean it.*

Farelli looked from Lucy to Jake with shrewd eyes. Glanced down at his ring. Careful here. The guy could smell a lie. Farelli licked his lips.

"I'm still listening."

Jake waited a beat. "It's not here. It's in Berdoo. In a safe deposit box. I don't have the key. It blew up with J—Tommy. But I can take you there." He hoped his slight stumble over his friend's name went unnoticed. *Damn, Jerry, what a mess you've left me to clean up.*

Farelli raised one brow. "I knew with the right leverage you'd tell me what I needed to know. But, I'm not going anywhere. I'm going to keep little Miss Down Time company back at the house, just in case you forget why you're on your way to Berdoo. You can take Marco and Civvy here with you on the private jet."

Shit, shit, shit. Lucy staying with Farelli? Not good. This was not good. She knew he was blowing smoke up Farelli's ass. That he had no idea where Tommy had stashed his take. Unless the Porsche was the sum of all his ill-gotten gains.

And then Lucy turned. Or rather, Farelli gave her a push, and she stumbled back between the two beef heads who'd been holding her earlier. She looked at Jake and simply blinked through those sexy glasses. She would be quiet. She knew the score. And she was counting on him to bring them home.

The two guards around Lucy stood at attention, waiting for their walking orders. With a nod, Farelli released everyone from their positions while he took hold of Lucy's arm.

Then he paused to speak over his shoulder.

"Oh, and Nicky?"

Jake raised his brows and winced from the sting of his open cheek.

"You have three and a half hours to fly there, get my money, and fly back. Otherwise I may just start a feminine finger collection. For every minute you're late." He winked at Jake and then he and Lucy disappeared through the plastic curtain, his entourage trailing behind.

Left alone with Marco and Cervantes—"Civvy," of all nicknames—while the service elevator lumbered upwards, Jake smiled crookedly and said, "Road trip." He then turned toward the elevator to push the return button, and his companions moved to either side of him.

He needed to get away from these two and fast. He'd said San Bernardino to buy himself some time, to get far enough away from the compound that he could take out these two schmucks. And then he would come back and rescue Lucy.

The captain had always said he was ballsy. It was time to live up to the reputation.

Chapter Seventeen

Lucy waited for Jake in Anton Farelli's sitting room, a prisoner in a gilded cell. The walls were covered in some swirly, golden wallpaper, and the sofa and chairs were covered in a crushed, gilt velvet. She had to admit she wasn't exactly uncomfortable. The couch she perched on was soft. Farelli had water and sandwiches delivered to her by the guard who now sat across the room in a straight-back, French-Provincial-style chair by the only door.

However, before he left, the creepy drug lord had taken one of her hands in his well-manicured ones and studied her fingers. And she knew right away what he was doing even before he gave her a grin with unbelievably white teeth. The intimidation had worked.

Now she was sitting. Sitting and waiting. Waiting for Jake Dalton to come roaring over the horizon with a SWAT team and tanks and helicopters. Even though he had left with an escort, she had no doubt he would return for her. Hadn't he told her with just one look that he would?

But as time wound by, misgivings crowded her mind. Yes, he'd told her he loved her. After they'd both been through a traumatic event. Had they simply been words spoken in the heat of the moment?

Her gut told her Jake had meant what he said. The way he'd said it, the way he'd looked at her, and the way he'd made love to her the other night, as if each time was their first time, served as proof. But she had learned over the years not to trust her gut. Too many Jobless Bobs had crumbled her self-confidence.

So she continued to doubt.

Whenever she looked up, she found the guard ogling her. It gave her the willies, the way his gaze would drift over her, pausing at her breasts and at her crotch. Every time their looks collided, he'd lick his lips, and she'd cover her mouth in the hopes of not throwing up. Would he go against his boss's wishes and attack her? She didn't know and didn't want to find out. *Please hurry, Jake.*

Besides his behavior, the guard carried a wicked-looking gun straight out of a James Bond movie. But he didn't resemble any 007 she'd ever watched on the big screen. Stocky and stuffed into a suit that looked two sizes too small, the man was more like a heavy-weight boxer. His facial features appeared smashed together, as though someone had stepped on his face with a size thirteen. She shivered and found herself wishing for an interruption, even from the evil Mr. Farelli, anything to keep the sleazebag across the room from approaching her.

But no one came, and her worst imaginings materialized. About an hour into her wait-time, she saw the guard rise from his chair. She tried not to watch him, kept track of him from the corner of her eye. With his gun in his right hand, he adjusted himself, and then swaggered toward her. Lucy jumped up and ran around behind the sofa she'd been sitting on, attempting to keep furniture between them.

"M...Mr. F...Farelli might come back here any minute," she warned, looking around for an escape route. Any way out. But the guy kept advancing.

"Nah. Women ain't his thing. Money is. He don't care about you. Besides, do you really think Mr. F's gonna let you and Costas free when Nicky comes back with the dough? If he even comes back. You're kiddin' yourself if you do, sweet cheeks."

Her knees wobbled at his approach. She backed up until her butt hit a table, rattling the objects on top of it. Was that what was going to happen? They would kill Jake as soon as he gave them the location of the box? The box that he'd made up in the first place? She would be naïve if she didn't consider it. The guard sauntered right up until their chests touched. Lucy grabbed the edge of the table behind her and swallowed the whimper before it escaped her throat.

"Even if Mr. Farelli doesn't care what you do, J—Nicky will kill you if you touch me." At the last minute she remembered only she knew Jake's real name. Oh, God, what was she going to do if this guy didn't stop? She wasn't about to get raped, not after everything else that had happened to her. She'd managed to keep safe all these years by herself. There was no way she was going to let herself down now. Since Jake wasn't here, she'd have to think of something, and fast, because the creep's expression told her he didn't care one bit what Jake would or would not do.

"I'm shakin'." He laughed, reaching up to run his hand over the sweatshirt covering her breasts. She batted his hands away. Quick as a wink, the guard snatched her hair and yanked, hard.

"Ow," Lucy cried, but bit her lip when he shoved his scowling face close and used his other hand to grope her. His skin shone with perspiration, and his breath smelled like garlic. Her stomach rolled from the odor and the realization that he was going to attack her if she didn't do something. Now.

"No bitch lifts a hand to me. Now, show me whatcha got under all those clothes." His rough hand fumbled at the bottom of her sweatshirt, and she stifled a scream. Who would come help the prisoner they were going to kill anyway? Nobody.

The jerk crowded her now, arching her backward over the table, and Lucy scrabbled for something, anything on that table behind her that she could use as a weapon. Her fingers brushed against something solid. She seized it.

He was snaking his hands under the sweatshirt, grabbing at her breasts, when Lucy took the object and swung it into his head. Hard. He toppled like an elephant. In reaction, great hiccupping sobs shook her whole body while she lifted her trembling arm to see what she'd used to club the would-be rapist. It was a brass statue of Hercules. How fitting. Dropping it beside the behemoth, she closed her eyes.

Within seconds, Lucy gained some self-control and swiped the tears from her face. Looking down at the big slob, she wondered if he was dead. If you struck someone right above the ear could you kill that person? Could she live with herself if she had?

No. She wouldn't worry about that now. She needed to think. To escape.

Now that the immediate danger had passed, the wheels in her brain began spinning again. This guy wouldn't have been locked in here with her. He would have had a key to the door. And a phone. She could free herself, maybe call 911, and then make it all the way out to a car. Not probable, but she had to try. What if they drove Jake out to the desert and shot him as soon as they found out he'd lied about the safe deposit box? That would be the horrible but logical next step, after all.

No, she had to assume she was on her own. If by some miracle they brought him back and she was gone, she could have the cops already on the way. But she had to search the disgusting guard for keys and a phone.

Ewww. The idea of touching him sickened her, but she forced herself to search him. His chest rose and fell—so he wasn't dead, more's the pity. But the lump on the side of his head guaranteed her a chance to escape the Farelli home. If she hurried.

She gagged as she felt along his chest and whimpered when she realized she had to go fishing in his pants' pockets. Just as she reached for his front pockets she heard a sound at the window and she spun around.

Crash!

She squealed, leaping to her feet as a figure broke through the window and began pushing all the golden curtains aside. *Not again*, she thought with rising hysteria. But then her eyes focused and she realized that the person tangled in all that fabric was none other than Jake. With ripped jeans and hair stiff with sand, he'd never looked dearer to her than at that moment. Without any hesitation, and unmindful of all the weaponry he had strapped on, she ran to him, giving him scant seconds to open his arms and catch her when she launched herself at him.

"You came for me, you came for me," she babbled, throwing her arms around his neck and squeezing his hips with her legs. She kissed his face all over, couldn't hear what he was trying to say over her frantic welcome. And then their lips met, and all speech was suspended.

Oh, God, he tasted like wind, and heat, and, yes, sand. Sand and safety. Security. She could have cried all over again, but she was done crying. And besides, he was returning her kisses, feeding on her lips like a hungry man, holding her head with one steady hand while she clung to his body like a second skin.

He drew back enough to look into her eyes. "Are you all right? I was so worried about you. I didn't know what they might do to you, how they would treat you—what happened to him?"

He was staring at the walrus on the floor, her almost-rapist. She swallowed. He would murder the man if she told him the truth, and she couldn't lose Jake to prison for that. She loved him too much.

"I...I wanted the keys," she hedged. "And...and his phone. I, uh, came onto him, and the rest was easy. I was just searching him when you jumped through the window." She made herself look innocent in the face of his scrutiny.

He looked down at the creep again and then back up at her, twice, before he finally said, "I don't think so, my pretty little liar, but we don't have time to argue. I didn't come in very quietly, so we've got to get the hell out of here. Now."

She let out the breath she'd been holding. He'd accepted her story even if he really didn't believe it and that was all that mattered.

He motioned her to the window. While she started toward it, Lucy saw Jake draw back his foot and kick the guy in the head. She pretended not to notice.

Jake looked out the window in both directions. Lucy stood as close as she could, trying to see around him and reveling in the warmth from his body, the safety he exuded just by being near her. God, she'd thought she'd never see him again.

He drew his head in, saw how close she was, and stole a kiss. It was way too short. She wanted to melt against him like ice cream in the sun, but she understood that time was short. She pouted just the same.

He grinned at her and said, "That's a down payment for later. You're all I thought about while I was gone, you know. Well, you and how to get these awesome guns from those douchebags. And now that I have them and you, well, I'm a happy man." He kissed her again and started out the window, saying, "Do what I do. The car's parked over that rise."

It wasn't far to the ground from the window, and soon they were both crouching in the sand while Jake scanned the area one more time. At last he looked back at her with another of his lopsided grins. "Follow me."

They took off along the wall, hunched over beneath the other windows spaced along the exterior. Up ahead, before they could break for freedom, was what looked to be a portico flanked by potted palms, with two black Mercedes parked under it.

Just as they came close, a door that she hadn't noticed

in the shade of the portico opened, emitting two black-suited linebacker types with bald heads and dark sunglasses. They talked rapidly, attention averted from this side of the driveway.

Jake stilled, raised a finger. Scared as a rabbit, Lucy flattened herself against the wall alongside him. Their shoulders touched. She felt hot, cold, and faint all at once. They would be dead if they were seen. They would be dead if they were seen. THEY WOULD BE DEAD IF THEY WERE SEEN. As she struggled not to panic, Jake turned his head toward her. And winked. She gaped at him, open-mouthed.

The two men crossed in front of the cars and opened a door to another part of the rambling house. As it swung shut behind them, Jake said in the lightest of whispers, "Three, two, one…now." He jumped up and they began their hunched run all over again. Lucy kept pace. It was all she could do, and it kept her from thinking of anything else. Like gunshots.

They reached the end of the house in under a minute. There was barbed-wire fencing ranging the perimeter, and she imagined more guards or dogs. Or cameras. She started looking around and, sure enough, she saw a camera on the corner of the building, just slightly above and to the right of them. It couldn't pick them up at this angle, but what about when they made a run for it? She turned to Jake, who was still crouched and also looking at the camera, studying it with narrowed eyes while it rotated.

"How are we going to get around that?" she whispered. For all she knew, the camera could pick up sound, too.

"Just like I did getting in. Carefully. I'm gonna go first, pull apart the fencing, and then you're gonna move that sexy ass over to me and crawl through. Piece of cake."

She stared at him. Was he out of his mind? They couldn't do all that in what? Thirty seconds?

"How long do we have between rotations? Half a minute? That's not enough time," she huffed, feeling more hysteria rising up.

Jake didn't help any when he replied, "It's plenty, sweetheart. I promise. Just do what I say. You trust me, don't you?" He sobered. All traces of humor and excitement were gone. In their place was concern. Concern and...doubt? Before she could respond, he continued in a lower tone, "I won't let anything happen to you, Lucy. You have my word. You matter more than anything else to me. I'll die keeping you safe."

She almost cried. Felt the welling of big, fat tears building behind her eyes. Gosh, she'd never been so watery in all her life. She wanted to throw herself into his arms, blubber about how much she loved him. Even opened her mouth to say it. But then he added, "So quit stalling and start running when I tell you to." Before her mind completely wrapped around one more of his lightning-swift mood changes, he glanced up at the camera and then took off. Oh, she could kill him.

His run across the sand to the fence was quick, and any other time she would have admired the way his legs pumped over the ground, how tight his butt looked in those jeans. But right now she kept looking up at the camera, and then back at Jake as he held the wire fencing and crept through it. When he fell to the ground and flattened out, she watched the camera. Not a moment too soon. It cruised over him, paused at the end of its cycle, and started back the other way.

"Now," she heard him order across the distance. She took off running toward him. He already had the fencing spread as wide as he could, and when she reached him she carefully crept beneath it. Once she was through, they both turned without speaking and slid down the slope toward the black Hummer he'd driven off in what seemed like days ago, but had really been less than two hours.

"What did you do to your two guards?" she asked, heading toward the passenger side.

"The same thing you did to yours," he replied with another of his grins. Then he continued, "Wrong side. You're driving. I need to be able to shoot. The highway's that way." He motioned to their right, but Lucy stood glued to the ground.

"I can't drive now," she said, shaking her head. She couldn't drive them from danger, from certain death. He was crazy.

He stopped close in front of her. "You can and you must. We will be followed, and you can't shoot a gun, but you can drive. You've kept up with me so far, Luce. Don't stop now. I've already called the cops. They're probably on their way. We're almost home free."

She studied his face, saw the bruises, the cuts that told the story of the last few days. And she also saw the care, the concern. And yes, the love he must feel for her. And she knew she could do this. For them. For him. She stood on tiptoe and brushed his lips with hers before heading around the hood to the driver's side. She could feel his gaze on her all the way.

Once inside the car, he asked as she started it, "You ready to blow this pop stand, sweetheart?"

Cocky Jake was back, and she hoped it was because of her kiss. She grinned right back at him. "Let's do this."

Chapter Eighteen

The Hummer bounded over the desert terrain like a boat sailing into the swells. Jake's head bounced off the roof of the SUV at regular intervals, but he dared not complain. They were laying Goodyear tracks away from danger and certain death. He just didn't know if he'd be able to get a bead on anything the way they were rocking and swerving.

He continued to steal quick little glances at his driver while he faced out the retracted rear window. He was trying to understand what had happened to her back at the compound that would make her club her guard like she was hitting to the fences. Lucy Parker was a pacifist by nature, he'd learned, so something major must have transpired.

Just then the phone he'd borrowed from Cervantes buzzed in his pocket. Well, the cat was out of the bag now, he decided as he ignored the incessant whine. Once Farelli didn't hear from either guard, he'd come to the right conclusion pretty damn quick and send reinforcements. Jake just hoped helicopters with rocket launchers weren't in Farelli's repertoire of weaponry.

"I think they're onto us, Lucy," he ventured, motioning to the shape of the phone in his pocket while shifting toward her. She threw him a panicked look.

"Just keep driving, sweetheart. It'll take them a while to circle the wagons. You're doing great."

"I want this over, Jake," she said with a catch in her voice, and he wanted so much to pull her into his arms and tell her everything would be okay. He could only hope to God it would be.

"We'll get out of this Lucy, just like everything else. We're survivors." He shot her a smile that she returned with a weaker facsimile. Encouraged, he poked gently, "Did that guy back there make some moves on you, Luce?"

The way her eyes shot to his and then skittered away told him more than her lukewarm, "Why would you ask that?"

"Because you're not the type to go banging guys on the head unless they deserve it. You can tell me the truth. We're far away now. Did he?"

They hit a nasty dip and Jake cracked his head against the ceiling despite the seatbelt. Swearing, he squinted at his driver. Had she done that on purpose to shut him up?

"We don't have to talk about it if you don't want to," he said. "You took care of him, and I know where he'll be if I want to look him up later." Oh, he'd look him up all right. Look him up with a couple of fists and a bat. By the time Jake was done with him the asshole would be an oversize doormat. Another wave of cold fury washed through Jake at the thought of that piece of shit touching his Lucy, let alone—

He inhaled sharply to control his imagination, his rage. He had to let it go for now. But when this was all over…

Unaware of the homicidal bend of his thoughts, Lucy offered a relieved, trembling-lipped smile, and he felt his anger seep away, felt like the sun shone only on him. Christ, if he hadn't already figured out he was in love, this would've been the moment for sure. When making someone happy meant more to him than his own happiness, he knew he'd found that one person who made him whole.

A black Humvee roared onto the roadway from their left. "Lucy, look out!"

Farelli had rallied his troops.

Lucy cut their Hummer to the right in a spray of sand. Tires spun and the vehicle responded instantly, shooting over the terrain. The pursuing Humvee was no slouch. It swerved back and forth in the rearview mirror, gaining on them.

"It's getting closer. What do I do? Jake, what do I do?" The Hallmark moment had evaporated in the wake of impending doom. Now Lucy screamed at him over the roar of their SUV's engine, zigging when the monster Humvee zagged, foot still pounding the accelerator. Jake put the Uzi's butt to his shoulder, sighted down it, and swore.

"Keep driving, Lucy. But for God's sake, try not to hit every friggin' rock in this desert." He couldn't count on hitting anything the way they were bouncing, and he didn't have unlimited ammo like he was sure the dudes back there packed.

"I can't help it," she wailed, and then squealed when gunfire erupted from the chasing vehicle.

"Punch it, damn it," Jake ordered, ducking as low as he

could and spewing off a few rounds in the general direction of their followers. "And stay down, for Chrissake. These guys mean business."

The other Humvee attempted a PIT maneuver, the driver trying to clip the rear of their vehicle to send it spinning out of control. Lucy stomped on the accelerator like Jake ordered, and the SUV launched out of the assault vehicle's grasp, fishtailing wildly. She screamed, scrabbling at the steering wheel.

"Straighten out…straighten it out, for God's sake, Luce! Ohhh, shit, here comes another one, they're like cockroaches. Move it…*move it!*" Facing backward, he began shooting indiscriminately while an identical menacing Humvee joined the chase, crisscrossing the other's path behind them. They returned fire. Lots of fire.

When he ran out of ammo in the Uzi, he threw it out the back window of their Hummer. It bounced off the hood of one of their pursuers, and Jake had a moment's satisfaction when the driver swerved. Too bad he came back, more pissed than before.

Lucy was screaming now. Jake had been wrong to put her in the cockpit, but he'd been right about the gunfire. He just didn't have enough rounds to fend off Farelli's troops.

"I don't know what to do," she chanted. "They're going to kill us. Help me, Jake."

Her panic was going to be their downfall if he didn't move his ass. Picking up his last weapon, an MP5, amidst more wild shots from behind, Jake took some calming breaths. He needed rock-steady hands for these next few minutes.

"Keep it together, Lucy. Hold the frickin' wheel steady

and just keep your foot on the gas. Do it." He sighted on the driver behind him, who immediately began weaving. The car giving them chase popped off more rounds that burrowed into their Humvee's steel sides.

Jake could hear Lucy whimpering while he held his breath, but then everything tunneled until all he saw was the driver behind him, snaking his car from side to side while his companion aimed at Jake. The other Humvee had dropped back, as if the two were tag-teaming them.

Jake took his shot, a spattering of rounds right through the windshield of the other Humvee. He was rewarded when the driver slumped over the wheel, and the vehicle went careening to the right, into the path of the other Humvee. Before they collided, Jake saw the passenger's mouth open as he realized what was about to happen…

The horrendous noise and ensuing explosion was nuclear. Glancing in his side mirror, Jake watched as the two vehicles erupted in a blazing fireball, accompanied by the ripping sound of screaming metal.

"Shit, that was freakin' awesome!" He settled back in his seat, grinning. But the Bonnie to his Clyde was ready to keel over. "Pull it together, Luce. The cavalry has finally come."

Lucy followed his gaze out the windshield. A long stream of cop cars, light bars flashing and sirens blaring, were racing toward them on the nearby highway. Slowing to a stop, she shifted into park, collapsed against her seat, and closed her eyes.

Unable to resist, he leaned over the console and kissed her on the lips, a new boyfriend's kiss that was more exploratory than sensual. When she opened her eyes, he reared back a little. "It's almost over, sweetheart. I told you we were survivors. But it's time for you to move on, and for me to help clean up this mess."

Tears tracked down her face. She reached out for him across the center console, awkwardly pulled him into her, and squeezed tightly. "I don't want to leave you, Jake. What if they don't believe you? You'll need my testimony—"

"Not if I can make a deal to keep you out of it." He set her back from him.

"I don't think this is right, Jake. I have a bad feeling about it."

He shrugged. "It's the only way, Lucy-love. I can bring down the whole house of cards, but I'm not doing it if you're involved. You matter too much to me. All you have to do right now is stay quiet and let me do the talking. And then leave. Trust me."

They stared at each other. Her lower lip began to tremble. He remained stalwart, though it about killed him to do so. Those sad, sad eyes peered out at him through cockeyed glasses. And she was still the hottest, sweetest, smartest woman he'd ever laid eyes on.

At last she swiped at her face. "You've taken care of me so far, I guess. What do I have to do now?"

He reached out to smooth her hair. Across the sand, a bullhorn-wielding officer of the law told them to "step out of their vehicle with their hands up." The rest of the cavalcade raced on toward Farelli's compound.

Jake tried to assuage Lucy's fear with a smile. After all, she'd never been involved in a police bust. He winked. To her question he said, "Watch and learn, sweetheart. Watch and learn."

Chapter Nineteen

Six Months Later

"Last four sandwiches, you guys. Two turkeys on sourdough, the other two beef halves with soup. Let's finish strong, folks."

The concerted "whoo-yah" from the kitchen staff brought a wide grin to Lucy's face. She grabbed two of the four plates and helped her wait staff distribute the final meals to the hungry lunch crowd waiting in the brick-walled space. Choruses of "ooo's" and "ahhs" met her delivery, and she paused to chat a moment with the recipients.

She found she enjoyed customer interaction even more than tallying the bottom line of sales at the end of every day. She'd certainly become a restaurateur in these last six months, and now there was no turning back.

After expressing her thanks for her customers' patronage, Lucy returned to the back of the kitchen, content to watch her crew finish up and start the shutdown process for the afternoon. She could afford a few moments of private gloating. Hadn't she handpicked this staff just so she could step aside and admire the well-oiled machine of her making?

"Another good day, Luce."

Lucy turned toward her friend and restaurant manager. "They're all becoming good days, aren't they?" At the woman's nod, Lucy continued. "You're not sorry you made the move then, Jane?"

Her friend shook her head and smiled. "Not sorry at all, Lucy. Just kinda wish you had a life outside of this place, too. You work all the time."

Lucy knew that. Work was all she had. But she'd grown these last six months. Grown as a small business owner and as an independent woman. She'd learned how to run a successful restaurant and continued to immerse herself in the operation of that restaurant, even if she'd relinquished the actual managing of the floor to Jane.

It had been a long road up to this point, since she'd walked into Matheson's office and tendered her resignation. Everyone at the firm had stared as quiet, dutiful little Lucy Parker of the navy skirts and sensible shoes cleaned out her cubicle, and drove away in a hundred-thousand dollar Porsche. Jaws had certainly dropped.

Turning to Jane now, she responded, "I go out with you guys all the time. Remember our Friday evening happy hours?"

"That's just with all of us at the restaurant. When's the last time you went on a date?"

Lucy froze. She looked past Jane, into her recent past. And remembered a night in a fancy Las Vegas hotel. Her handsome companion with the Renaissance man good looks and the twenty-first-century smart mouth. That mouth...

Shaking away the memories, she returned to the present, schooling her expression into the pleasant mask that covered her feelings. She'd become a master at concealing those true emotions. Jane would not be getting past her outer armor today. Gazing at her concerned friend, Lucy replied in a quiet tone, "Two Hearts takes all my time right now, Jane. You know that. I'm not in the market for a man. Been there, done that."

"You can't wait forever, Lucy. He's not coming."

Lucy squared her shoulders. "Begging your pardon, but I'll be the judge of that. Let's just drop it." She'd never told Jane much about Jake. Only that he had some unfinished business to take care of. And that she wasn't ready to date yet.

Jane patted Lucy's shoulder. "Dropping it right now. I'm going back to box up the leftovers for the shelter, okay?"

Lucy nodded. At least her friend hadn't taken offense. There were just some topics Lucy couldn't broach yet, and love was one of them. There wasn't a day that went by that she didn't relive the moments she'd spent with Jake Dalton.

Why didn't he come? He'd said he loved her, yet here she was, running a restaurant by herself that she'd bought for him with her retirement nest egg, sleeping in a new, king-size bed alone, waiting for him to make her whole again.

Lucy stared at the supply racks of the restaurant she'd romantically named the Two Hearts Café, as a stubborn refusal to admit defeat within the boxing ring of love. It had been six months, six long months of no word, yet she refused to give up hope of ever seeing Jake again. Her heart wouldn't let her.

They'd both been taken into custody that day in the Las

Vegas desert. Separated and questioned endlessly. Jake had initially refused to talk to anyone, but Lucy hadn't. She'd cooperated with the law because she wanted to make sure Farelli and his entire outfit remained behind bars. She didn't want to have a hit on her if they slipped through the cracks and got released because of something she didn't divulge.

At last she had been allowed to leave, but had been told that Jake was going to be detained for in-depth interrogation by both his department and the FBI. She flew home to wait for him there. She was sure he would come for her when he straightened everything out. He'd told her he would.

When those first months passed by and Farelli's arrest and incarceration hit the news, she called the police station where Jake had worked. No response. She'd left messages. Spoken to other detectives, dispatchers, his boss. Even the deputy chief. She'd received the same answers from bored, disinterested voices. Jake Dalton couldn't come to the phone. Jake Dalton wasn't available. And finally, Jake Dalton *wouldn't* talk to her. That last statement sliced her heart in two, and she wondered how she was still alive, how that organ continued to beat.

And that was when she decided to move on with her life, to stop living in cheap motels because she was afraid to return to her little apartment. The apartment where Delano/Fisk had attacked her so brutally and Jake had expressed an interest in her.

She'd learned that life could change in a heartbeat and could be snuffed out just as quickly. And that if you loved someone, you'd do anything for that person. Like open a restaurant for him.

In the manner of that movie, *Field of Dreams,* Lucy

hoped that if she took her savings and used it for Jake, he would come. So she'd gone to her bank, took out all that money she'd been accumulating for a rainy day, and promptly began spending it.

She'd moved out of her little home that had been violated, taking what she needed and sending the rest to charity. She'd found a quaint little apartment above a vacant restaurant in the Mission Inn Square of downtown Riverside. She'd gotten her hair styled and bought designer glasses that flattered her face more than the mall optometrist's brand. All with the idea that she wanted to look her best when Jake showed up.

She set up an account to deposit a small stipend every month in her mother's bank account. She told her mother that if she ever begged or pressured for more, the payments into her account would stop. It was the perfect threat.

And lastly, because she was tired of being dependable, boring Miss Lucy Parker, of the navy skirts and sensible shoes, she walked into her boss's office and summarily quit. Then she went out and bought the restaurant below her apartment, because again, if she built it, he would come.

It had been rough at first, since she had no clue how to be a restaurateur. But she Googled "how to run a restaurant," took a couple management classes at the community college, and then dove in. She became so busy she nearly forgot her broken heart, until the wee hours of the mornings, when she woke for no apparent reason with tears on her cheeks and an ache in her chest. But she'd thrown herself into getting the sandwich shop off the ground, and soon the pain nearly subsided. Nearly.

After she added an online catering business, Two Hearts

became so popular that Lucy wooed her friend Jane away from the accounting firm to help. The two women ran the businesses into the black, seeing positive money flow straight to their respective bank accounts.

If not for the lack of Jake in her life, she would have been the happiest person on the planet. She was at last living her life exactly the way she wanted. She answered to no one but herself, and realized that she could stand on her own two feet without the presence of a man in her life. But she still wanted one man.

She read the newspaper accounts of the Farelli drug ring being broken, read that the drug lord would die in prison appealing his case, which had yet to be heard. She looked for news of an inside informant. Nothing. Not a mention of Jake. Or herself. He'd dropped out of her life, if not her memories.

It just figured that when she finally fell in love, the road to happily ever after refused to be wide and clear. Oh, no. She would be the one person run off that road, left at its side to hobble back into single-hood.

The jangle of the restaurant's front door announced a latecomer who was ignoring the sign that said the café was now closed. Sighing, she made her way to the front counter. Before she even rounded the doorway, she pronounced in her most official voice, "We're closed now. We don't serve dinner. Sorry. If you'd like to come back tomorrow—"

"I want the manager's special. Lucy Parker to go."

She ground to a stop, head bouncing up at the gravelly-voiced announcement. When she met the sparkling, sardonic, brown eyes of the speaker, all the menus slid from her lifeless hands.

It was Jake. Standing before her in her restaurant.

Smiling at her as if it had been twenty minutes since they'd last spoken, and not six, long, heartbreaking months. Looking sexier than ever, with collar-length, dark hair combed back neatly from his forehead, and just a hint of stubble covering his chin and riding his upper lip. That body she'd loved to touch covered in thigh-hugging denim and a long-sleeved, plaid shirt.

She stared at him across the space. And remembered all the calls she'd made to him, all the calls that had been denied. The messages that had told her he wouldn't talk to her. The responses that had cut her to the quick with their coldness.

"You didn't answer my calls." She saw something like remorse flicker in his eyes. She took a steadying breath. "You never once called me. All those months I waited for you, and not once did you let me know how you were doing, what was happening."

"I told you it would be a colossal—"

She gave a jerk of her head. "You could have at least talked to me!" Her voice rose at the end. Horrified at the amount of hurt she felt when this reunion should have been happy, Lucy spun around so he couldn't read the emotions on her face.

"Oh, hell, Luce," Jake cursed. He strode around the counter and, taking her in his arms, pulled her tight against his body even though she stiffened at his touch. His hands stroked her hair. Smoothed down her back in an attempt to comfort, yet she remained ramrod straight within his arms. He whispered, "I'm sorry. So, so sorry," over and over, kissing the top of her head between apologies.

But the warmth of his body and the sound of his voice

seeped past the barrier she'd erected against the pain of his rejection. This was Jake, and he was here. Whatever he'd done or hadn't done these past months, he was still Jake, and she still loved him. So she wrapped her arms around his neck in a stranglehold and burrowed into the comfort of his arms.

"You hurt me, Jake. When you wouldn't talk to me, you hurt me. I didn't know what was happening, and I missed you so much. I thought you'd left me for good."

He rocked her back and forth. "I told you it would be a mess, Lucy. I had to fight long and hard to get them to believe me. I broke a lot of laws. I killed a federal agent, remember? And then, during all this bullshit they were slinging at me, the weirdest thing happened. I received an envelope in the mail from a bank in town. I must have been the beneficiary on an account Jerry set up. When I checked into it, guess what I found?"

Not really listening, still stunned that Jake was here, holding her, Lucy shook her head against his chest.

"A hundred-thousand dollars."

That caught her attention. She pulled back in his arms. He was grinning. Grinning and nodding. "Yep, it was Jerry's take from Farelli. I stared at it for at least five minutes. Even expected the IRS to jump out at me and say 'Gotcha!'"

"Wh—what did you do with it?"

"I handed it over to my captain. It sure as hell helped exonerate me, since the bank clerk identified Jerry as the one who'd taken out the box. So here I am. My department and the feds cut me a deal. *They* effed up and listened to information from a murdering madman for over a year. They had to take accountability for their own mistakes. I love you, sweetheart. I was always coming back to you."

He'd come for her. He'd been cleared, and he'd come for her. After so many sleepless nights, so many tear-filled, lonely days, he'd returned. Jake Dalton had come back to her, and he'd said he loved her.

After those words she'd been dying to hear for all these months, she raised her eyes. They coursed over his beloved face, noting the long, dark hair with no more ugly red and the crinkle lines at the corners of those beautiful brown eyes. She found worry, maybe even insecurity, in their depths. What did he have to worry about? Didn't he know she'd loved him all this time?

At last she spoke, her voice hoarse. "So you're free? No jail?"

"Yes, Ma'am. I was offered the Golden Finger with full twenty-year retirement benefits, even though it hasn't been twenty years, and I took it. They'd screwed me over royally and it was their way of making amends. I will have to testify, and my retirement hasn't kicked in yet, but I'm free.

"Crime fighting has lost its appeal for me. When you can't tell the good guys from the bad, and you lose faith in the system, it's time to take a hike. So I did. Question is, have you moved on with your life? Have you…met someone else? When I didn't talk to you and I left you with so much time…maybe you figured you wanted someone new?"

Ah, so now the lack of communication made sense. She cocked her head as realization dawned. He'd handed her the chance to find another man. He thought she'd give up on him. That she'd tire of waiting for him. But he didn't know her heart like she did. Because even though she might have moved on in her mind, her heart, her one-man-forever heart, had still held out hope.

And then the new Lucy, the independent, sexy Lucy with the designer glasses and studio haircut, the one who could fight off a drug dealer and open a new restaurant all by herself, had an idea. A surefire way to convince this wonderful, vulnerable man that her feelings for him had never waned.

She reached out and grabbed his hand. She turned to the stairwell and yelled to Jane, "Lock up, Jane. I'm going up," and towed him behind her up the stairs.

Spring's early evening shadows fell across the bed in her brick-walled apartment over the Two Hearts Café, making it appear later than it actually was. Foot traffic in the square below, with its accompanying voices, drifted up through the opened windows of the bedroom.

With her head resting on Jake's shoulder and one hand rubbing along his smooth chest, Lucy decided that talking was highly overrated.

Their actions over the past hour had spoken the volumes they'd been unable to say. The tender way he'd held her, the hesitant, reverent way in which he'd made love to her, had told her more than all the words in Webster's dictionary how much she meant to him. And she'd shown him just how much she missed him, loved him, and needed him in her life. She wanted to show him again, actually.

"You keep doing that and you're gonna wake him up." His voice rumbled lazily under her ear. That was exactly her objective. Jake had returned to her, had at long last shown his feelings, and she couldn't get enough of him. She had to celebrate their love. So she continued with her hand and leg coordination exercises, until he made good on his prediction and rolled on top of her.

He stared down into her eyes and she felt her head spin just from being in his arms again. It would always be that way with him.

"I want *you* awake. I don't want to waste another moment apart. I love you, Jake." Her voice was thick with emotion.

Holding her gaze, he slid into her, and Lucy was complete. She pulled him close, close enough to feel his heart beating against hers. Close enough to hear his voice rumble in his chest.

"Then marry me, Lucy Parker."

She blinked. He'd asked her to marry him. *He'd asked her to marry him!* After all this time apart, after all the months of tears and loneliness, he'd come back into her life and asked her to marry him. She didn't even have to think about it.

Craning upward, Lucy began raining kisses all over his beloved face, punctuating each with a gleeful "Yes!" She felt him heave a sigh, and marveled that he'd been nervous about her answer. Silly man. She shifted beneath him, and only then did he begin to move within her, slowly at first.

Without breaking eye contact he increased the tempo until that familiar tension began to build. And then, just before they reached the brink, he lowered his mouth scant inches above hers and whispered, "I love you, Lucy Parker."

It was the start of their forever. Together.

The End

Acknowledgements

Special thanks go to my editor, Vanessa Mitchell, for seeing the potential of the story and not resting until she pulled the best out of me. You are my mentor.

Thank you also to Katie Clapsadl, my publicity editor, for setting me up for success in the social media world.

Thank you to my very good friend Pat Elliot, who helped me find just the right word in many an instance. Your vocabulary knows no boundary!

Lastly, a special thank you goes to Orange County Sheriff Clay Cranford, who spent time explaining undercover investigation procedures to me. He went above and beyond, so any mistakes or inaccuracies within the book are purely my own.

About the Author

Cathy has always loved writing, but that pesky thing called Real Life cast writing into the backseat for years. Now she has reunited with her creative passion, and devotes every moment she can to all the plots and characters milling about in her imagination. She admits she finds story plotlines in everyday occurrences going on around her.

When she's not writing her special mixture of romance and humor, she likes to travel, read, and take long walks with her husband (the inspiration for her happily-ever-afters). Cathy looks forward to many years of writing for readers' enjoyment.

Made in the USA
Lexington, KY
21 May 2017